EVERY WITCH WAY BUT WICKED

A WICKED WITCHES OF THE MIDWEST MYSTERY
BOOK TWO

AMANDA M. LEE

WINCHESTERSHAW PUBLICATIONS

For the real Wicked Witches of the Midwest
Long may they reign with grace, terror and even a whole lot of sarcasm.

ONE

"*He* looks like he's naked a lot."

The statement took me by surprise. I had no idea who Edith was talking about, but I was suddenly interested. I didn't bother looking up from the file I was looking through at my desk, but I did tune in a little harder with my ears. Of course, I tried to pretend like I wasn't listening – mostly because I didn't want Edith to think I was shallow, well, any more shallow than she already thought I was.

"He's not naked a lot," another voice scoffed. "He's a businessman. The only time he's naked is in the shower – like it should be. He even keeps his socks on in bed."

I still wasn't used to the other voice yet. It was relatively new – and old – at the same time.

I glanced up to see Edith regarding the new denizen of the paper with one of the most skeptical looks in her repertoire. "Do you really believe that?"

For his part, William Kelly had the grace to look abashed. "Probably not," he finally ceded. "He's a good-looking boy. It's not his fault the ladies throw themselves at him."

I watched as William tried to sit in the chair across from my desk. Instead of sliding into the chair comfortably, though, I noticed that he was floating about two inches above it. Since he was a ghost and he'd only been dead for a little less than two weeks – this was a pretty solid accomplishment (pun intended).

Edith, on the other hand, looked like she was actually making contact with the other chair. She'd been dead for a lot longer than William, so she'd had more time to practice.

"He is good looking," Edith mused, smoothing her slate gray hair with her hand. It was a nervous gesture she'd retained from life. As a ghost, there really wasn't any hair there to put into place. "What's wrong with him?"

"What do you mean?" William looked confused.

"Isn't he like thirty? Shouldn't he be married by now?"

I tuned the two ghosts out again and glanced out my office window in the direction where their gazes were trained. I internally sighed as I caught sight of Brian Kelly, the new owner of The Whistler, the only newspaper in Hemlock Cove. He really was good looking. With his blond hair, chiseled jaw and sparkling blue eyes, he couldn't be considered anything but gorgeous. Still, there was something about him I just didn't like. I didn't say that out loud, though. After all, he was William's grandson.

My name is Bay Winchester and, yes, I see ghosts. I've been able to see them for as long as I can remember. I can hear them. I can talk to them. And, no, it no longer freaks me out – much.

Why can I see ghosts? I was born with the 'gift.' Unfortunately, there was no return policy on being a genetic freak. You see, I'm from a long line of witches. We all have some special abilities. One of my cousins can see the future, and one can read minds – sometimes. My mom and my aunts were all accomplished kitchen witches – and I had a feeling they all had other 'gifts' that they weren't exactly making public. That was actually good, because I had no inclination to know what they were truly capable of.

Then there was my Aunt Tillie. Actually, she was my great aunt, but since I was raised in the same house with her, that distinction was never really set in stone. There are no words to describe Aunt Tillie – even though 'evil' and 'batshit crazy' spring to mind on occasion.

I shook my head as I tried to break from the reverie I had momentarily lapsed into. This wasn't the time to think about Aunt Tillie. If I started thinking about her now, I would drive myself to the brink of insanity – and then find myself in a blind rage. I was still mad at her. More on that later, though.

Instead of dwelling on Aunt Tillie and her latest exploits, I turned my attention back to Brian Kelly. He was getting the two-cent tour of The Whistler. He had just inherited the weekly paper from the former owner, William, when he died. Brian was one of William's grandsons. According to William, he was the only one left in the family capable of running the paper, so he had inherited by default.

I didn't point out to William that he hadn't been technically running the paper for the past five years. I had. I didn't want him to see exactly how bitter I was about his grandson coming in and vowing to 'shake things up.' This was Hemlock Cove, after all; there wasn't a lot to shake up.

Hemlock Cove is a small town in Northern Lower Michigan on the west side of the state. There is minimal access to Lake Michigan and maximum farm acreage and dense woods. It could be interchanged with just about any other town in the immediate area except for one thing: It was a town of witches.

Okay, the majority of 'witches' in Hemlock Cove weren't really witches. In fact, the only witches in Hemlock Cove who would know an actual curse if it bit them in the ass (that happened to me once thanks to Aunt Tillie) had the last name Winchester. Still, a couple of decades ago, the town found itself at a crossroads. It was faced with a dwindling manufacturing base and a seasonal tourist population in the summer and the winter. Something had to be done.

The town leaders decided to rebrand the town as a tourist destination year round – and they settled on making it a place for paranormal delights. In truth, the rebranding really consisted of installing cobblestone streets, quaint and kitschy shops, dressed-up townspeople and old-school bakeries and restaurants – all the while hiding any trace of technology. Still, the rebranding worked.

Tourists now come to Hemlock Cove year round – although fall is our busiest time of year – to ride horses, tour corn mazes and just imbibe cider and homemade whiskey to their heart's content.

I had been serving as editor of The Whistler for five years. I grew up in Hemlock Cove, but I left for a few years to become a journalist in Detroit. My time spent in the city wasn't a waste, but I was happy when I returned to the open air and home. The news might not have been as earthshaking, but the scenery was prettier and the people were a lot more welcoming – for the most part.

A few weeks ago, though, I had gotten a surprise when the city – or at least the crime -- had visited Hemlock Cove in the form of a big meth bust and two brutal murders. The murders had ended with something of a supernatural twist, which I was still trying to wrap my brain around.

Surprisingly, despite the stir the drug bust and murders had created in our small hamlet, life had returned to normal relatively quickly. That was before William died, though, and left the paper to his grandson.

From what I'd been able to find out on Google, Brian Kelly was a real estate developer from Ohio. He had been born in Hemlock Cove, but left with his mother when he was ten. He had only been back sporadically since.

"What do you think he wants?" I finally asked William.

"What do you mean? He wants to make this paper the best in town," William looked nonplussed.

"It's the *only* paper in town. By default, that makes it the best paper in town," I pointed out.

"Well, maybe he just wants to put his stamp on it," William shot back.

I frowned in response. I had a bad feeling this wasn't going to work out well for me. I had become accustomed to a certain level of autonomy under William's leadership. I wasn't looking forward to giving that up.

William must have noticed my sudden discomfort. "Don't worry. I made keeping you on as editor part of the agreement for him taking over the paper."

I looked up at him in surprise. "You did?"

"Of course," William waved me off. "What does he know about running a newspaper?"

I was relieved by the news, but still wary of Brian's presence at the paper. It was a small building. I had a feeling his ego was going to take up a lot of space.

I looked to my door expectantly as I saw Brian step to the entrance. He knocked, even though he saw me looking at him through the plate glass window. That was at least considerate. I waved him in and plastered a fake smile across my face. "Back again, I see?"

"Yeah, I'm just trying to get a feel for the building," Brian said, flashing me a dimpled smile as he took a seat in one of the chairs across from my desk. Since he was now sitting on Edith, I couldn't help but feel a little uncomfortable.

Edith jumped out of the seat, scandalized. "Well, that's just rude."

I steadfastly ignored Edith and William. If I didn't, Brian would think I was crazy – and no one needed that at this point in our relationship. I'd had a lot of practice pretending I didn't see ghosts growing up, so it wasn't that hard.

"It's not a very big building," I said with a small chuckle. "There's not a lot to get used to."

"No, but I was just looking at my grandpa's office and figuring out what I wanted to do with it," Brian admitted. "I loved my grandpa, but he had awful taste in office furniture."

"Those are antiques," William practically shrieked. "He better not just throw that furniture out. That furniture is worth more than his car."

I bit my inner lip in an effort to keep the laugh that was bubbling near the surface from escaping. William's outrage was cute, though. It was a hard battle.

"I think he was pretty attached to that furniture," I said finally.

"Yeah, I'll make sure it finds a good home," Brian said.

"That's good."

We lapsed into an uncomfortable silence for a few minutes. I wasn't sure what to say to him. I didn't want to encourage him to get too comfortable making editorial decisions, so talking about this week's edition of The Whistler was definitely out of the question. Besides, I didn't think the two-page preview of Hemlock Cove's upcoming Murder Mystery Weekend was going to send him into an excited frenzy.

"It's almost lunchtime," he said.

"Yes," I said. What else are you supposed to say to that?

"I thought maybe you could give me a tour of the town and then we could talk business over lunch? I'm buying, of course."

Crap. That was the last thing I wanted to do. "I'm supposed to have lunch with my cousins at Hypnotic," I said. It wasn't exactly a lie; we had lunch together at their mystical store at least three times a week. We had nothing set in stone today, but they wouldn't be surprised to see me. "You're welcome to have lunch with us." The invitation was merely out of courtesy. I didn't figure he would accept it. I was wrong.

"That sounds great," he said enthusiastically. "I've been wanting to meet some of the area business owners. Might as well start at the top."

I smiled at him openly, but inside I was cringing. My cousins, Thistle and Clove, weren't exactly the top businesswomen in town. If he approached them in the wrong way, they would eat him for lunch.

On second thought, that might be fun.

"Let's go."

TWO

*H*emlock Cove is picturesque, no matter what time of year you visit. Autumn, though, has a special type of magic. Not only are the leaves turning, making the downtown more colorful than usual, but the town actually smells like brewing cider thanks to all of the stores that serve it this time of year.

I smiled to myself as I led Brian down the cobblestone street. I watched as his head swung from storefront to storefront. Main Street is a cornucopia of visual stimulation in the fall. The Halloween decorations give it a slightly ominous feeling – especially given the murders a few weeks ago -- but most of the tourists are exhilarated by the decorations more than anything else.

As we walked, Brian asked me questions about certain stores. I told him about Mr. Wharton's hardware store, Mrs. Gunderson's bakery – best pumpkin rolls ever made, I swear – and Mrs. Little's pewter unicorn store.

"There's a whole store dedicated to selling pewter unicorns? That can't be profitable," Brian laughed.

"You'd be surprised by what is profitable in Hemlock Cove," I chortled. "This isn't a normal town, in case you haven't noticed."

"No, I noticed," Brian smiled warmly. "I just didn't realize that you could actually make a profit selling pewter unicorns."

"Mrs. Little is one of the richest women in town," I reminded him. "She does more than make a profit. She makes a killing."

I paused outside of Hypnotic and waited for Brian to catch up. I noticed that Thistle and Clove had gone all out this holiday season. Thistle, an accomplished artist, had even painted the front windows of the store with a garish tableau of witches and vampires. I glanced over at Mrs. Little's front window, which was decorated with paper cats and sparkly witches, and smirked to myself. The dark picture Thistle had painted must be driving her crazy. It was a short trip, though. That's what made it so much fun.

"This is your cousins' store?" Brian asked, looking at the window painting appreciatively. "Did they have to hire someone to do this? It's pretty impressive."

"No, Thistle did it," I said simply. "She's pretty talented."

"I'll say."

I led Brian into the store. My cousin Clove was standing behind the counter bagging herbs. She looked up when she heard the wind chimes at the door tinkle signaling our entrance. Her long black hair was tied into a loose braid at the nape of her neck. At only four-eleven, Clove is diminutive in size but big in attitude. She seemed surprised to see that I had a guest with me.

For his part, Brian hadn't noticed Clove yet. He was busy looking around the store, taking in the homemade candles, the variety of herbs and an entire stand of home oils.

Clove raised an eyebrow in question, but she didn't say anything. My family isn't exactly known for thinking before speaking, but Clove was 'trying something new.' A week ago, our other cousin, Thistle, had accused her of being a blabbermouth. In an attempt to prove she was not a blabbermouth, she'd been making a concerted effort to think before she spoke. The plus side was that she hadn't blabbed any secrets in a week. The downside was that she often forgot what she wanted to say while she was thinking of what *not* to say. I didn't think her new endeavor would last that long. Truth be told, I actually missed her chatterbox nature.

I watched Brian look around for a few minutes, but I was starting to get impatient. "Where is Thistle?"

"She's in the back," Clove said carefully. "She's doing work."

I smirked to myself. I could tell by the way Clove was biting her inner lip that Thistle was not working. She was probably mixing potions – but Clove didn't want to say anything witchy in front of Brian.

"This is the new owner of The Whistler, Brian Kelly," I introduced him to Clove.

Brian tore his gaze from the shelf of wax skulls Thistle had made last week and greeted Clove with a bright smile. "This place is great."

"Thank you." I could see Clove blush a little. She was obviously attracted to Brian's good looks. Of course, Clove's attractions usually lasted about five minutes, so I didn't know if she was in this for the long haul.

"Who made the skulls?"

"My cousin, Thistle," Clove answered. "I thought they were a little garish, but they've been selling really well."

"I bet."

"So, you're Bay's new boss," Clove said. I saw her dimple come out to play. She had listened to me complain for two days straight about having a new boss. I hadn't told her how good-looking Brian was. "You're not what I expected."

"What did you expect?"

"Someone older," Clove said honestly. *Someone less attractive*, I mentally supplied. If Clove picked up on my projected thought, she didn't let on. "So what do you think of The Whistler so far? Bay's doing a good job, huh?"

"She's doing ... the best with what she has," Brian said finally.

Clove's frown mirrored mine. What was that supposed to mean?

"What is that supposed to mean?"

Clove, Brian, and I all turned in surprise as Thistle exited the back of

AMANDA M. LEE

the store and entered the front display room. Her short-cropped hair was dyed a violent shade of purple – a mix between lilac and fuchsia actually – and it brought out the warmth of her skin tone. After six weeks of blue hair – which Thistle's mom, Twila, swore up and down made her look like a twisted clown – Thistle had finally broken down and changed the hue. In truth, Thistle had grown tired of the blue after a few weeks. She'd kept it for another three weeks just to irritate Twila. She had just dyed it purple the night before. I couldn't wait until the rest of the family saw it.

"You must be Thistle," Brian greeted her warmly.

Thistle didn't return the smile. "What did you mean when you said that Bay was doing the best with what she had? This is Hemlock Cove, not Detroit. She can't manufacture stories." The tone of Thistle's voice was deadly.

"That's what I meant," Brian said sheepishly. He could sense the sudden shift in the room. We were a pretty impressive force – especially when we all had PMS.

Clove was suddenly nervous. "I don't think he meant anything bad by it," she supplied.

"How do you know?" Thistle challenged.

"I don't. I was just ... don't be a pill."

"A pill?" I raised my eyebrows. "Have you been spending time with the aunts?"

"I don't know why I said it," Clove grumbled. "It just came out."

I walked over to the comfortable couch in the middle of the room and slid into it. I spent as much time on that couch as I did on the one at the guesthouse where the three of us lived together. It was housed on the property of The Overlook, a local bed and breakfast run by our mothers. And, no, they still didn't get the irony of renaming the inn after the creepy hotel in *The Shining*.

"Brian wanted a tour of the town," I said, trying to break the frosty silence that was still emanating from Thistle.

Thistle shot one more dark look in Brian's direction and then made her way to the couch and plopped down beside me. "Why is he here?"

"He wanted to meet local business owners," I replied. "He wanted to start at the top."

Clove glowed under the compliment. Thistle merely softened – slightly. "What do you want to know?"

Brian sat down on the chair across from us. I couldn't help but notice that it was the furthest sitting surface from Thistle. She was fairly frightening when she wanted to be.

"I just wanted to get a feel for the town, and the business owners," he said smoothly. He flashed a sexy smile in Thistle's direction. I didn't have the heart to tell him that it was entirely wasted on her. Even if Thistle wasn't in a constant state of flirt with the local stable owner, Marcus, Brian wouldn't be her type. She's Bohemian chic, not business casual.

"The town is pretty set in its ways," Thistle said, her tone blithe. "The town has an identity that isn't going to shift. Even if you want it to."

"Why would I want it to shift?"

"You just have that look about you," Thistle challenged.

"I love the town," Brian replied. "I can't imagine a cooler place to live."

He said the words earnestly, but I don't think any of us – even Clove – believed him.

Clove decided that the best way to ease the tension was food. We all agreed on Chinese, and Clove placed the order. It would be twenty minutes before the food arrived, and we were all stumped for a topic of conversation.

If it was just the three of us, we would have talked about the revenge we were currently plotting on Aunt Tillie for her latest curse – which Thistle was convinced had given her a mustache. That wasn't really an option, so we settled on the upcoming Murder Mystery Weekend that the town was hosting.

"This is the first time the town has done something like this?" Brian asked.

"We do a lot of town events, bonfires, and reenactments," Clove explained. "This is the first time we've done a murder mystery that everyone is involved in. We have events all week leading up to the actual murder mystery this weekend."

"Do you know who the murderer is?"

"We're not on the planning committee," Thistle said wanly. "Our mothers are, but they won't tell us what is planned."

Brian chuckled throatily. "Don't they trust you?"

"Not even a little," I said ruefully.

"Sounds like a fun family." He was shooting for levity.

"Only if you're into masochism," Thistle shot back.

Brian searched all three of our faces for traces that Thistle was joking. I don't think he was encouraged by the grim set of all of our jaws.

"I can't wait to meet the rest of your family," he said finally.

"Famous last words," Thistle muttered.

THREE

*A*fter lunch, Brian made a hasty exit. He said he wanted to introduce himself to a few more business owners, but I think he really just wanted to get away from Thistle.

The truth is, Thistle is often grumpy – but she's usually not overtly hostile. Planning revenge on Aunt Tillie had been consuming her for three days straight. I don't think she'd been getting a lot of sleep.

I promised Brian I would meet him back in the office a little later in the afternoon, but I wanted to talk to Thistle and Clove about some things before I returned to the office.

"You just want to gossip about my dimples," Brian said charmingly at the door.

Clove blushed when his gaze landed on her. I flashed him a fake smile. I could tell Thistle was fighting the urge to shoot him the finger.

When he was gone, I turned to my cousins. "What do you think?"

"I think he's an ass," Thistle said simply.

"I think he's hot," Clove sighed dreamily.

"I think he's up to something," I interjected.

"Like what?" Thistle asked suspiciously.

I shrugged. "I don't know. I just get a weird vibe off him."

"He's probably evil," Thistle said.

"He's probably just a nice guy who spent a lot of time in the city and is out of his element," Clove corrected her.

"You're so naïve," Thistle grumbled.

"And you're so ... witchy," Clove's voice had risen an octave.

"We're all witchy," I smirked.

"Keep an eye on him," Thistle warned me. "I don't trust him."

"You don't like him," Clove countered.

"It's the same thing."

We lapsed into silence for a few minutes and then I turned to Thistle expectantly. "So, what do you have planned for Aunt Tillie?"

"I haven't decided yet," Thistle said stiffly. "It's got to be epic, though."

"I'm still not sure she cursed us," Clove said, her doubt evident.

"We all grew mustaches overnight," Thistle scoffed. "Do you remember what waxing them felt like? It hurt. Then they didn't grow back, although you had what looked like razor burn on your upper lip for a week. That's definitely a curse."

Clove frowned. "I still don't understand why I had such a bad reaction to the wax."

"Probably because she was really mad at you," I said. "And she took it out on all of us to make a point."

"I told you, I am not the one that stole pot from her field," Clove challenged. "I think it was Twila."

"It doesn't matter. She thought it was you because you looked stoned that night."

"My eyes were red from the pollen in the air," Clove practically shrieked.

Thistle and I watched Clove suspiciously. Neither one of us were sure Clove wasn't actually the one who had stolen from Aunt Tillie's pot field. We hadn't even known about the field until a couple of weeks ago. In the time since, Clove kept going for 'walks' in the middle of the day. None of us were especially known for hiking through the woods, so you can understand our suspicions.

"I'm not going over this with you again," Clove said stubbornly. "It wasn't me. Maybe it was the two of you and you're just blaming it on me?"

Not likely.

"You know Bay and I get our life highs from a bottle, not from herb," Thistle replied snottily.

"Only a guilty person tries to push blame off onto someone else," I supplied.

"I hate you both," Clove grumbled.

Thankfully for all of us, the door at the front of the store jingled. We all turned to see a handsome man walk through the door. He was dressed in simple jeans and a white T-shirt, but you could tell how impressively built he was thanks to the snugness of both.

"Hi, Marcus," I said sweetly, shooting a glance in Thistle's direction. I couldn't tell for sure, especially because she had on so much makeup, but I could swear her cheeks were reddening.

Thistle and Marcus had been flirting for a month. Marcus was now running the town stable, and Thistle was suddenly interested in picking up feed for the inn's horses on a regular basis.

They hadn't gone out on a real date yet – but it was only a matter of time.

"Hello, ladies," Marcus greeted us amiably. "You all look especially pretty today." His gaze fell on Thistle – and lingered there. "Your hair looks amazing."

Thistle smiled at him, unconsciously smoothing her ankle-length floral skirt, while steadfastly ignoring the teasing grins Clove and I were shooting in her direction. "Thank you. You don't think it's too much?"

"No, it is really flattering," Marcus said honestly.

He really was sweet. When you paired his warm personality with his hot body, shoulder-length dirty blond hair and pretty face, the overall package belonged on the pages of a fashion magazine – and not in Hemlock Cove.

Thistle was struggling for words, and the room had lapsed into an uncomfortable silence, so I decided to try and help her. "Did we forget to pay our bill, Marcus?"

"No," he hedged.

"Did you need something from the store?" Clove asked helpfully.

"No."

Clove and I exchanged humorous glances. Did he want to mount Thistle in the middle of the retail herb section? "Can we help you with something?"

"Um, I was just wondering if maybe Thistle wanted to go to dinner tonight." He said finally.

Clove and I both turned to Thistle expectantly. We'd been waiting for this development for what felt like years.

"I'd love to," Thistle said hurriedly.

"We have dinner at the inn tonight," Clove reminded her. Actually, we had dinner at the inn several times a week, but we'd been informed that tonight was mandatory attendance because of the upcoming murder mystery planning.

"Crap," Thistle grumbled.

"You could have dinner at the inn with us," I offered, shooting a devious look in Thistle's direction. "The aunts would love to have you there. They love feeding people."

Marcus looked caught, and Thistle looked murderous. "You don't have to," she said lamely.

Marcus squared his broad shoulders, ran his fingers through his sun-streaked hair, and smiled at Thistle decisively. "I would love to have dinner at the inn."

"You would?" Thistle looked stunned.

"I've heard a lot about your family," Marcus said. "I want to meet them."

That wouldn't last long.

"Dinner starts at 7 p.m.," I told Marcus. "Don't be late."

"I won't," he said. I could tell he was suddenly nervous as the reality of the evening ahead of him started to set in. "I can't wait."

The door to the store had barely shut behind Marcus when he left and Thistle was on me. "You're dead to me."

This wasn't especially surprising. We all killed one another off at least once a week. "You'll get over it."

16

"Or she'll just get even," Clove interjected.

That was a sobering thought. I didn't have time to dwell on it long, though, because the door was jingling again. Marcus couldn't have changed his mind this quickly. Could he?

Instead, we all saw Brian enter the store again. I was surprised he managed to find his missing testosterone so quickly.

"Did you forget something?"

"No, I just wanted to ask if you guys know of any place good to have dinner. I thought you could join me and we could talk about the newspaper. We never got to talk over lunch, after all." The request was pointed, but I wasn't feeling particularly persuaded by his sudden reappearance.

"I have family dinner," I said apologetically. "Attendance is mandatory."

"You could come to family dinner," Thistle said suddenly. So much for being dead to her.

"Where is family dinner?" Brian looked confused.

"Up at The Overlook," Clove said. She was smiling at Brian again. Great.

"The inn? That's where I'm staying until I find a place," Brian looked pleased. "That sounds great."

Double crap. I kept my silence until he left the store again, promising he wouldn't be late for dinner. Then I turned to Thistle grimly. "I hate you."

"You'll get over it," Thistle said brightly.

"Your night is still going to be worse than mine," I reminded her.

"How do you figure?"

"I'm not planning on sleeping with Brian. The aunts will take one look at you and know it's only a matter of time until you get naked with Marcus."

Thistle's faux brightness faded quickly. "This sucks."

This definitely sucked.

FOUR

I went back to the office after arguing with Thistle for a few more minutes. Neither of us was giving any ground, so it was a pointless fight. We both had to conserve our energy for tonight anyway. Aunt Tillie would smell blood in the water when both Brian and Marcus showed up – and that blood would equate to weakness – and that weakness would turn her into the shark from *Jaws*. We would be chum in the water if we weren't careful, and there wouldn't be a boat big enough in the world to save us if Aunt Tillie felt like she could move in for the kill.

Brian didn't return to the office – for which I was thankful – but I couldn't get a lot of work done with William and Edith nattering on about everything under the sun. I figured Edith was just happy to have someone to talk to. If ghosts could flirt, I think that's what she was attempting to do. It was a painful endeavor to watch, though.

For his part, William was still getting used to his new situation. I still hadn't figured out why he was a ghost at all. Most ghosts either die a violent death and stay until their murders are solved – or they have unfinished business. I didn't want to press William on it yet – especially if he was hiding some sort of hidden trauma. I had my own problems to worry about right now.

I packed up my laptop after two hours of staring at an empty screen and headed home. I dropped my belongings off at the guest-house where Thistle, Clove and I lived and changed my clothes quickly.

The guesthouse is a three-bedroom abode that is completely self-contained. It has its own kitchen, living room, and a full basement. It only had one bathroom, though, which made mornings a pain when all three of us were trying to get ready at the same time.

The guesthouse was located on the property of the family inn – which had undergone a massive renovation a few months back. The inn could house a number of guests, and it had a formal dining room and reading room for the general public. It also had a private residence at the back of the property where my mom, her two sisters, and our great-aunt lived together. The only way you could get to the living quarters from the main inn was through the kitchen – which no one ever tried because Aunt Tillie was so frightening.

While I was changing in the bedroom, I heard the door to the guesthouse open. "Why are you changing before dinner?"

I walked out into the main room in time to see Thistle cast a disdainful look in Clove's direction. "I just want to look nice."

"For Marcus?"

"For myself," Thistle snipped back.

Clove slid a sly look in my direction and then threw herself on the couch to wait. "Don't take too long. It will just give them fodder – and you don't want to give them any more ammunition than they already have."

Despite Clove's warnings, Thistle took a full twenty minutes to get ready. Her efforts were worth it, though. When she came out of her bedroom, Clove and I both whistled appreciatively at her ensemble. She'd changed into an ankle-length gypsy skirt in a lovely lavender hue that complemented her new purple hair. She had also put on a sequined black tank top that managed to show off an impressive amount of cleavage. She looked hot. Her mother was going to have a fit.

I glanced down at my simple jeans and T-shirt and wondered

briefly if I should change. I didn't want Brian – or anyone else, for that matter – to think I'd changed for him, though, so I opted to remain as I was.

We walked the 500 yards up to the inn and let ourselves in through the back door. The family living quarters are decorated in bright colors, and there are a variety of different floral concoctions on the walls. To the casual observer, it would look like three women liked dried flowers and herbs. To anyone familiar with the craft, though, it would look like four practicing witches had erected an impressive array of protection spells and wards.

Most of the town knew there was something off about the Winchester women – and many had guessed that we were actually witches. Guessing and proving, though, were two entirely different things.

When we got inside the living room, none of us were surprised to find Aunt Tillie sitting in her favorite chair watching *Jeopardy*. The fact that she was wearing sunglasses indoors was something of a surprise, on the other hand. I opened my mouth to ask the obvious question and then snapped it shut. Not only is it a bad idea to inter-rupt *Jeopardy*, but it's also a bad idea to give Aunt Tillie an opening when you don't have to.

Instead, I merely shook my head and continued through the living quarters until I reached the kitchen. As suspected, my mom and aunts were busily cooking dinner – and chatting away amiably. None of them looked up when the three of us entered the kitchen.

"You're late," my Aunt Marnie admonished, not looking up from the asparagus she was chopping.

"Thistle had to change her clothes."

Thistle shot me a death look, which I steadfastly ignored. I figured it was better that Thistle be the center of their wrath instead of me. I love my cousins, but I'm willing to sacrifice them to the family beast whenever possible to save myself.

Clove wandered over to Marnie and dropped a kiss on her cheek. Seeing them together must be a sobering thought for Clove, I thought briefly. They looked exactly alike. They were both short – right around five feet – and they both had pitch-black hair (which I knew Marnie was getting from a bottle these days to hide the gray). They were also top heavy – for lack of a better description. Seriously, they were stacked. Marnie repeatedly teased her less endowed sisters by actually sitting them on the table from time to time.

Thistle hopped up on the kitchen counter and snatched a slice of apple from my mom as she was sliding the cut fruit from the carving board into the homemade pie shell on the counter. My mom smacked Thistle's hand dismissively – but there wasn't a lot of force beyond the motion.

"That's for dessert," she admonished Thistle sharply.

"Aunt Winnie, you know I love your apple pie," Thistle said charmingly. "You can't expect me to wait for perfection, though."

What a suck-up.

My mom slid a knowing look in my direction. "At least someone appreciates me."

Good grief.

I glanced over at my Aunt Twila, Thistle's mom, to see what she was doing. I couldn't be sure, but it looked like she was basting stuffed chicken breasts. Yum. She hadn't looked up from her task yet, but I couldn't wait until she did. When she saw Thistle's new hair color things were bound to get interesting.

Twila finished her basting and slipped the chicken breasts back in the oven. She straightened and then turned to greet us. Her mouth dropped and her eyes flew open when she saw Thistle's new hair. "What did you do?"

"I dyed it," Thistle said coyly. "I thought you would like it. You'd been nagging me for weeks because you didn't like the blue."

Twila pursed her bright red lips – which matched her own distinct hair color -- and regarded her offspring dubiously. "When I told you to dye your hair, I meant to a more natural color. What's wrong with your own hair color? It's beautiful."

The truth was, I couldn't exactly remember Thistle's real hair color anymore. We had pictures from when we were kids, but for as long as I could remember, Thistle had been changing the hue of her hair whenever the mood struck – and her moods were usually the brightest shades of the rainbow she could find in a bottle at the local head shop.

I had a sneaking suspicion that Thistle's love of changing her hair color had as much to do with her own taste as it did with irritating her mother. Hey, we've all done it.

Of course, for Twila to discriminate against anyone's hair was pretty rich. I had no idea what her natural color was either, mostly because I had never seen it. She'd had the same bright red hair since I was born – and the shade of red she opted for couldn't be found in nature. It could be found on the creepy clown from *It*, though.

"I thought you would like the color better," Thistle said snottily. "Perhaps you should be careful what you wish for from now on?" Thistle quirked her dark brow suggestively. She really was ready for battle tonight.

Twila wasn't known for walking away from a fight either, and I could tell things were about to get ugly so I changed the subject. "Why is Aunt Tillie wearing sunglasses in the house?"

My mom bit the inside of her cheek and went back to her pie preparations. Twila suddenly found the dishes in the sink more interesting than the conversation. That left Marnie. I turned to her expectantly.

"Aunt Tillie has a condition," Marnie said carefully.

Clove looked up in surprise. "Is she okay?"

Thistle and I were more suspicious. Aunt Tillie was a lifelong hypochondriac. If she ever had a real condition, I wasn't aware of it. That is, unless you count vindictiveness as a physical ailment.

"She's fine." Mom dismissively waved off Clove's concerns.

Marnie arched her eyebrows. "She thinks her eyes are allergic to oxygen."

What? "I don't understand."

"Neither do we," Twila said cautiously. "It started yesterday. She says her eyes can't be exposed to oxygen."

I shot Thistle a curious look. "But sunglasses don't stop oxygen from getting to your eyes – and why would she possibly think that she's allergic to oxygen?"

"Because she's crazy and she wants attention." I think Thistle meant for the statement to be quieter than it was, but everyone in the room had heard – and given the sharp intake of breath from the older women in the room -- I had a feeling this was one of those things we weren't supposed to bring up around Aunt Tillie.

"Who wants attention?"

Everyone in the room froze at the sound of Aunt Tillie's voice. Crap. Today's episode of *Jeopardy* must be over.

We all turned to see Aunt Tillie's frightening figure – all four foot eleven of it – as she stood in the doorway. Well, everyone that is, but Thistle. She appeared to be trying to make herself smaller on the countertop. She was like a cat – she figured if she couldn't see Aunt Tillie, then Aunt Tillie couldn't see her either. What? It's a theory.

"My mom was just telling us about your condition," Clove said. I think she was trying to help Thistle, but it was obviously the wrong move.

"And Thistle thinks I'm making it up for attention?" Aunt Tillie's voice was ominous as she ran a hand through her close-cropped slate gray curls. She kind of reminds me of a hobbit some days – a really mean hobbit, but a hobbit still.

No one in the room spoke – or made eye contact.

"So everyone thinks I'm making it up for attention? You all think that an 80-year-old woman – the 80-year-old woman who has taken care of all of you for your whole lives – is making up a painful and debilitating ailment to get attention?"

She was pulling out the big guns now. Aunt Tillie only called attention to her age when she wanted to guilt us. When we called attention to her age to modify her behavior she was equally offended.

"Why do you think you're allergic to oxygen?" I asked finally.

"I'm not allergic to oxygen," Aunt Tillie scoffed.

Well that was good news.

"Only my eyes are allergic to oxygen."

Criminy. "And why do you think that?"

"Because my eyes have been watering for days and they're red and inflamed. When I wear the sunglasses and don't go outside, that solves the problem. What else could it be?"

Allergies. "It's fall, there's a lot of pollen in the air for the changing of the seasons."

Aunt Tillie gave me a withering look. "You sound like my doctor."

"And don't you think the doctor would know about things like this?" I know better than arguing with Aunt Tillie – but I can't help myself. Now I'm the cat and her paranoia is catnip.

"Not if it's a new condition that hasn't been discovered yet," Aunt Tillie informed me haughtily.

"And you think you're the first person to have this condition?"

"I've always been a scientific anomaly," Aunt Tillie shot back. "The sooner you people realize that and stop questioning my uniqueness, the better you'll all be."

With those words, Aunt Tillie flounced back out of the kitchen.

It was going to be a long dinner.

FIVE

*C*love, Thistle, and I helped carry all the dishes of food out to the dining room – leaving my mom's pies on the countertop to cool. When we got into the dining room, I noticed that both Brian and Marcus were already seated next to each other. That didn't surprise me, the rest of the guests at the inn were primarily couples.

The conversation at the table was light – and most everybody was excited about the upcoming murder mystery.

Everyone took their seats. I couldn't help but notice that Thistle had slid into the chair next to Marcus. His eyes had nearly popped out of his head when he saw her outfit. I didn't blame him.

Twila saw Marcus' gaze wander down to Thistle's cleavage – and she didn't look happy. I didn't know what she expected. Thistle had purposely brought out the big guns – well, as big as she could muster – for a clear purpose. She seemed to have achieved that purpose.

"Who is this?"

Aunt Tillie had entered the room and her gaze had immediately found Marcus. Thistle introduced Marcus to everyone at the table. My mom, Marnie, and Twila had met him casually at the stable – but Aunt Tillie didn't believe in manual labor, so she hadn't had the pleasure yet.

"You brought him to family dinner for your first date?" Aunt Tillie seemed surprised – and somewhat proud of Thistle. "You're braver than I thought."

After everyone had doled copious amounts of food onto their plates, the only sounds that could be heard were the various compliments being thrown around. My mom and her sisters basked under the attention. They were all accomplished cooks – and they were constantly in competition with each other to claim the title of 'best in the family.' If someone didn't like their food, it was considered a personal attack.

After a few minutes, Aunt Tillie fixed her attention on Brian. I had purposely picked a seat that was as far away from him as I could manage. "Who are you?"

"Brian Kelly, ma'am," Brian stood to extend his hand in Aunt Tillie's direction. She regarded it like he'd offered her a dead frog – although she probably would have liked that better.

"The man taking over the paper?"

Brian must have realized that Aunt Tillie wasn't going to take the proffered hand so he retracted it and sat back down in his chair. "Yes, ma'am. I'm Bay's boss at The Whistler."

"I'm sure she must be thrilled by that," Aunt Tillie said, her voice sarcastic.

If Brian picked up on the sarcasm, he wisely ignored it. "I have a lot of plans to improve The Whistler."

"Like what?" My mom bristled. "I think the paper is perfect the way it is. Bay does a wonderful job." The women in my family are irritating, but loyal to a fault.

"Of course she does," Brian tried to placate my mom. "I just think the paper could be more than it is."

"How is that?" Marnie asked. "It's not like this is a hotbed of crime and political corruption."

Brian looked confused. "I know but … ."

"It's not like Bay can manufacture the news," Twila interjected. "She can only report what's going on in the community, and this is a very small and tight-knit community that likes things the way they are."

"I didn't say that it wasn't … ." Brian said.

"What is it exactly that you're saying then? How do you figure that you can change the paper in a community that doesn't want to change?" Aunt Tillie was on the offensive. For my part, I was happy just to sit back and watch the show.

"I just think there is more news here than anyone probably realizes," Brian was feeling attacked. It was obvious. I didn't blame him.

"What news? You think we're all hiding some dark underbelly that only you can find?" My mom was incensed.

"No," Brian protested.

"You think that you somehow know this community better than Bay does – even though you haven't been here in years?" Marnie fixed a hard stare on Brian.

"No."

"You think that somehow you're going to magically come to town and turn the paper into some big daily that is full of nothing but crime stories and petty town fights? Like a gossip rag?" Twila asked.

"No."

"Then what do you think you're going to be able to do with the paper that Bay hasn't already?" Thistle asked irritably.

"I don't know," Brian said carefully. He was treading softly at this point. The room had taken a decidedly chilly turn.

"Then maybe you should stop talking out of your ass," Aunt Tillie sniped.

My mom turned on Aunt Tillie. "Don't be rude."

"What? I don't trust him," Aunt Tillie sniffed.

For once, we were on the same page.

THE REST of dinner was uncomfortable, but my mom and her sisters managed to convince the rest of the guests that the fireworks were over. I couldn't help but notice that Aunt Tillie was shooting disgusted looks in Brian's direction on a regular basis – even with the ever-present sunglasses affixed to her round face.

When dinner was over, my mom left two pies in the dining room for the guests, and took another two to the den located off the main entryway in the inn. We were meeting several people from the town to discuss the murder mystery plans and dessert would make things more pleasant.

I wasn't surprised to see that Chief Terry, the head of the local police department, was already seated in the den. He was an imposing figure, standing nearly six-feet tall, and his uniform and graying temples gave him a distinguished look.

Chief Terry was a regular fixture at the inn – and it wasn't just because my mom, Marnie and Twila were locked in a battle to secure his undying love. I couldn't be sure, but I think he got off on their subtle squabbling. Plus, the fact that they chose to battle with food items was just an added bonus in his book.

I caught a glimpse of Thistle at the front door. She was talking to someone. My guess was Marcus. She closed the door to the den when she entered the room, shooting me a 'butt out' look when she saw the question on my face. The interrogation would have to wait until we were back at the guesthouse.

"Marcus seems nice," my mom said to Thistle.

"He is," Thistle averted her gaze.

"Will we be seeing more of him?"

Thistle looked horrified at the thought. "I think our next date will just be the two of us," she said finally.

"That's probably wise," Aunt Tillie said knowingly. "You don't want to scare him off." Aunt Tillie looked Thistle up and down. "Although, if that hair didn't scare him off you're probably all right."

I choked back a laugh.

"What are you laughing at? Your date is an ass."

"He wasn't my date," I shot back. "He was a guest at the inn and Thistle is the one who invited him to dinner as payback to me for inviting Marcus."

"You're learning," Aunt Tillie said to Thistle before turning her attention back to me. "You should learn to stay out of your cousins' business."

"Like you stay out of our business?"

Aunt Tillie narrowed her eyes. "I am not a busybody."

Whatever.

"You should be glad to have someone with my vast knowledge working on your side," Aunt Tillie informed me.

"Except you're usually working against me," I grumbled. "Ow!" I confronted my mom angrily. "Why did you pinch me? That hurt."

"Don't start a fight with your aunt," she admonished me. "If you drag out this meeting longer than it has to be, then your aunt isn't going to be the only one cursing you."

Chief Terry looked surprised at my mom's statement, but she easily deflected his curious glance. "I made apple pie, would you like a slice?"

"Apple pie is my favorite," he said appreciatively.

"I know," my mom said, shooting Marnie and Twila a triumphant look. For their part, they didn't look especially terrified by her pie seduction powers.

We all looked up when the door to the den opened and Mrs. Little – the town's pewter unicorn aficionado herself – entered the room. "Sorry I'm late," she said apologetically.

"No one missed you," Aunt Tillie muttered.

Marnie shot Aunt Tillie a murderous look. The truth was, none of us liked Mrs. Little. She was a mean little gossip – and she didn't like us any more than we liked her. The problem was, we had to work with her if we were going to participate in any of the town activities because she was almost always the primary organizer. This wasn't the time to antagonize her.

Mrs. Little was still sharp – her suit choices notwithstanding – and I had no doubt she had heard Aunt Tillie's dig. "Tillie, so good to see you," Mrs. Little said with fake enthusiasm. "It's especially nice to see you when you're not poisoning the coffee at the senior center because you lost a hand of euchre."

Uh-oh. I had just recently found out that while I was out of town and working in Detroit, Aunt Tillie had created quite the stir at the senior center when she poisoned the community coffee with belladonna because she was convinced they were all cheating her.

"So, what do we have planned for the mystery weekend?" I broke in smoothly.

Chief Terry shot me a grateful look. He had been the one who opted not to press charges against Aunt Tillie. I had a sneaking suspicion it was because he didn't want his food supply cut off more than anything else.

Everyone turned to the task at hand. And, while the meeting was understandably tense, things managed to progress easily enough. Essentially, numerous members of the town were going to be 'killed off' by an unknown assailant over a three-day period. Town visitors were to follow the clues to the killer. Whoever solved the crime would win a special basket of goodies from the town's various businesses. Granted, it wasn't a great prize, but people were interested in the mystery and the ambiance of the town more than anything else.

"So, who is the murderer?" Thistle asked.

"None of your business," Mrs. Little said. "Only a handful of people know, and you're not one of them."

Thistle grimaced. Under normal circumstances, she would have unleashed a tirade of snarky comebacks. No one wanted to prolong the meeting, though.

"Who is dying? Or is that a secret, too?"

"We had hoped we could use Tillie as one of the deaths?" Mrs. Little looked at Aunt Tillie expectantly.

Oh, this was going to go over well.

"No."

"No?" Mrs. Little looked surprised.

"No. I don't want to be a murder victim."

"Aunt Tillie, we promised someone from the inn would serve as a victim. And since all three of us are so busy all the time ... ." Twila seemed hesitant to continue.

"No," Aunt Tillie crossed her arms over her chest obstinately.

Clove stifled a giggle.

Mrs. Little looked at my mom expectantly.

"We'll talk to her," my mom promised.

Mrs. Little took advantage of the break in conversation and excused herself. Once she was gone, I turned to my mom. "You're not going to get her to agree."

"You don't know that."

"I know that she's not going to play a convincing murder victim. She's not going to be able to just lie there and be quiet. We all know that."

My mom considered my statement seriously. "You're probably right."

"I'll do it," Twila suddenly volunteered.

Marnie groaned. Twila always did fancy herself a big screen actress stuck in a small town. Actually, I thought it was a pretty good idea. So did my mom. "Okay," she agreed. "After you die, though, you're going to have remain in the kitchen and the residence until after the mystery is solved."

"No problem," Twila said enthusiastically.

Thistle and I exchanged unconvinced looks. Twila wasn't exactly known for being under the radar.

The look wasn't lost on Twila. "Don't you two start your looks. I will be the best dead person in the history of Hemlock Cove."

Thistle opened her mouth to say something sarcastic, but I kicked her in the shin. "You can let some of them go, you know?'

Thistle rubbed her shin ruefully. "I'll try. She's not going to make it easy, though."

One look at Twila practicing dead stares from the floor told me that Thistle was probably right.

SIX

The next morning came far too soon – especially when the first thought that entered my mind was the fact that I would have my first full day of work with Brian Kelly and his massive ego ahead of me. Ugh.

I contemplated pulling the covers back over my head and hiding from the day, but after three minutes of trying to settle back into sleep, I knew that wasn't going to be possible. I really had to go to the bathroom.

With a dramatic sigh – it's genetic – I climbed out of bed and made my way into the kitchen for a cup of coffee. Thistle was sitting at one of the stools having her morning cup of coffee. She looked as cranky as I felt.

"Morning," I mumbled.

"Morning."

I poured myself a cup of coffee and slid onto the stool next to Thistle. Her short-cropped purple hair was standing on end. I thought about making fun of it, but I doubted my shoulder-length blonde hair looked any better so I let it slide. "What are you doing today?" I asked finally.

"Work," she grunted.

"And after work?"

"What do you mean?" Thistle was being purposely evasive. I knew that meant she was hiding something. If I had to guess, that 'something' had longish blond hair and a ridiculously hot body.

"So, you're going out with Marcus tonight?"

"How did you know that?"

"I guessed. I saw you two talking at the door last night. It wasn't exactly a stellar first date – what with our family, well, existing. I figured you'd want to get an *actual* first date out of the way before he realized what kind of gene pool we sprung from."

Thistle barked out a laugh. "Isn't that the truth?"

"So, what are you guys doing?"

"It's Hemlock Cove," Thistle shrugged. "There isn't a lot to do."

"So, you're going to the kickoff bonfire party for the murder mystery?"

"Pretty much."

Thistle sipped her coffee and then turned to me. "Is this your first day of real work with Brian?"

"Yeah."

"What are you going to do?"

"What do you mean? I'm going to shower and go to work."

"About Brian? You're going to have to put your foot down with him. He's too gung-ho."

"I think he'll figure out pretty quickly that he's not going to get what he wants from Hemlock Cove. It's not like we're suddenly going to have a huge crime problem or something," I replied.

Thistle looked doubtful, but held her tongue. She had her own day to worry about.

When I got to work, I wasn't surprised that Brian was already at the newspaper – or at least his car was in the parking lot. I dropped my laptop in my office and went to find him in his grandfather's office. He was pulling down portraits and stacking them against a wall.

"What are you doing?"

Brian jumped when he heard my voice. He swung around and

seemed relieved to find me standing in the doorway. "Sorry. You scared me. I was just taking these portraits down. They're not really my style."

"You seem jumpy," I pointed out.

"It's just that ... I thought I heard something a while ago. Like someone else was in the office. When I went to look, though, I was alone. It's like there's ghosts here or something," he said with a hollow laugh.

I glanced over at the leather wingback chair positioned against the far wall. William was sitting in it with his arms crossed obstinately across his chest. I had a feeling that he had been voicing his distaste with his grandson's redecorating efforts pretty vocally. I was impressed that Brian managed to pick up on that, though. Most 'normal' humans had no idea that another plane of existence even existed, let alone that we were intermingling.

"Are you sure you want to make big decisions right now? About redecorating, I mean?"

Brian looked confused. "Why not? It's my office now. It's not like my grandfather would care that I changed his office around. It's not like he can see it or anything."

"Ungrateful little cur," William growled from the corner.

I ignored William, which wasn't easy because his frustration was almost comical, but I didn't want Brian to think I was crazy.

"Well, I'll leave you to your redecorating," I said. "I'm going to go get some work done."

"What's this week's edition going to be?" Brian asked the question, but he never took his attention away from his current task. I had never seen anyone so obsessed with office redecorating before.

"The murder mystery, obviously."

Brian nodded distractedly. "Good. Keep me posted."

I left the office feeling like I had been dismissed more than anything else. When I got back into my office, I found Edith waiting for me. "William is very upset," she announced.

"I saw him."

I sat down at my desk and opened my laptop. Past experience had taught me that Edith was just getting started, and there was no way to stop her when she got a full head of steam.

"I can't imagine having such an ungrateful heir."

From what I knew about Edith, she had been something of a loner. When she died, she hadn't left any survivors but some distant cousins. It didn't surprise me that she didn't get the nuance of family.

"I think Brian is just trying to prove he belongs here," I explained. I had no idea if that was actually the truth, though. I was still getting a weird vibe from him I couldn't exactly give a name to.

"You don't prove you belong someplace by destroying everything that was already there," Edith said pragmatically.

She had a point.

"Besides, William came back to this place for a reason, because he felt drawn to it. He's not going to even recognize it when that idiot is done tearing it apart," Edith sniffed.

I looked at Edith probingly. "Why is William here?"

Edith furrowed her brow. "You mean, why is he at the paper? Or why is he a ghost?"

"Both."

"You'll have to ask him," she said evasively.

"Ask him what?" I almost yelped in surprise when William popped through the closed door and entered the room.

"Bay wants to know why you're here," Edith said simply.

"Here at the paper? It was my business and I loved it," William answered.

I decided to ask the question I'd been avoiding since William had popped back up at the paper more than a week ago. "But why are you here? Why are you a ghost?"

William shrugged. "I don't know. I went to bed one night. When I woke up, I got out of bed to get ready for my day and then I realized that I may have gotten out of bed, but my body was still there."

I chose my next words carefully. "William, most people don't become ghosts when they die."

"They don't? Why not?"

"Most people just move on," I explained. "They know they don't have anything left to accomplish on Earth, so they move on to what is beyond."

"To Heaven?"

"I don't know. I guess." I had never really taken the time to ponder the next life. Just thinking about it gave me a headache.

"So, why didn't I move on?"

"I don't know," I admitted.

"Why didn't you move on?" William turned to Edith.

"Because I still don't know who killed me," Edith supplied.

"You were killed?" William's eyebrows nearly shot off of his forehead.

"Weren't you?" I asked him.

"I don't know. I thought I just died in my sleep. Didn't the coroner say it was a heart attack?"

"Actually, I don't think the coroner did a full autopsy," I admitted.

"Why not?"

"You were ninety, William," I pointed out. "There were no signs of foul play. I think everyone just assumed you ... just died of old age."

"I'll have you know, I was in great shape," William said petulantly.

"I'm sure you were."

"At my last doctor's visit, my doctor told me I had the body of a man twenty years younger."

"So you don't know how you died?"

"No."

"Do you think you were murdered?"

William considered the question seriously. "I don't think so," he said finally. "Who would want to kill me?"

"You had a lot of money," Edith pointed out. "Maybe Brian wanted his inheritance now, instead of later?"

I watched William to gauge his reaction. He shook his head. "I had money, especially for Hemlock Cove, but I wasn't rich. Plus, Brian had no idea I was leaving him the paper."

"Who did he think was going to get it?"

"I don't know," William shrugged. "But it's not like the paper is a money machine. It makes money, but not enough to kill over."

I had seen the books. I knew William was telling the truth. The profits from the paper led to a comfortable living – in Hemlock Cove – but not enough to make someone rich.

"Sometimes people become ghosts because they have unfinished business," I said pointedly. "Is there something that maybe you felt like you hadn't finished?"

William's eyes shifted to the left as he shook his head. "No, absolutely not." With those words, William stalked back out of the office through the wall. You didn't have to be a good judge of character to know that he was lying.

Even Edith, who was oblivious to just about everything that didn't concern her, noticed the sudden shift in William's attitude. "He's hiding something."

He most definitely was.

SEVEN

*A*fter a couple of hours of work, I decided to break for lunch. I could still hear Brian busily moving furniture in the far office. I debated inviting him to lunch out of sheer courtesy, but I decided against it. I didn't want to spend time with him when I didn't have to.

The town was abuzz with energy as I made my way to Hypnotic. Everyone was out decorating the storefronts and streets, and preparing the central square for tonight's bonfire and kickoff party.

Hemlock Cove is always interesting, but when the town is planning a party, things are even more entertaining. I couldn't help but laugh to myself as I saw Mrs. Little bossing around several other business owners from her position in the middle of everything.

"That doesn't go there, Trent," she barked at a teenage boy. I think he was the grandson of the local hardware shop owner, Mr. Wharton. "Do I have to do everything myself?"

When I got to Hypnotic, I found Thistle and Clove busy with their own reorganization project – and a verbal spat.

"I didn't say they were ugly," Clove argued, waving at me as I entered. "I said I thought they were *garish*. There's a difference."

"You say garish, but you mean butt ugly," Thistle argued.

"I did not say that. I just think they're creepy."

"What are we talking about?" I asked, throwing myself onto the couch to watch them work.

"Clove says my new candles are ugly," Thistle said angrily.

"I didn't say they were *ugly!*" Clove was clearly at the end of her rope.

"Where are the candles?"

"In the box on the counter," Clove said.

I wandered over and looked in the box. Recently, Thistle had been experimenting with different types of candles. Clove had balked at the simple skulls Thistle had been manufacturing over the past two weeks. Thistle was apparently getting more creative with the skulls – if the candles in the box were any indication.

I pulled one of them out and couldn't help but laugh out loud. It was still a skull, but Thistle had fashioned ornate knives jutting out from them. The wicks of the candles were at the hilt of the knives. She had also colored what appeared to be blood at the base of the knives.

"Awful, aren't they?" Clove asked.

Actually, I thought they were kind of cool. "I bet they're big sellers for the murder mystery weekend."

"Which is exactly why I made them," Thistle said haughtily.

"You made them to irritate me," Clove countered.

"That was just an added side benefit," Thistle said snidely.

I put the candle back in the box and went back to the couch. "You guys want to order lunch?"

"We saw you coming down the street and already ordered sandwiches," Clove said. "It should be here in twenty minutes."

"Cool."

Thistle looked up from the herbs she was bagging and regarded me. "How was your first day with Brian?"

"I barely saw him," I admitted. "He's renovating William's office."

"That was quick," Clove said.

"Tell me about it. William is pissed."

"He's still hanging around?" Thistle asked. "Have you asked him why?"

Thistle and Clove didn't have the same gift I did. They couldn't see ghosts. We had found out recently that if I was in close proximity with them, they could actually hear ghosts – but neither of them was exactly pleased with that discovery. Thankfully, William hadn't made his way down to Hypnotic yet. He had been a beloved member of the community in life. Unfortunately, he was sometimes the dirty old uncle people try to hide at family reunions. Let's just say he had wandering hands.

"I asked him today," I admitted.

"What did he say?" Clove asked.

"He doesn't think he was murdered."

"Wouldn't he know?"

"Not necessarily. He says he went to sleep and just didn't wake up."

"And Chief Terry didn't order an autopsy?" Thistle asked.

"Why would he? William was ninety and there were no signs of a struggle or anything," I reminded her.

"Yeah, I can see why he wouldn't waste the time or money," Thistle grudgingly admitted.

"Something else weird happened, though," I said.

"What?"

"I asked him if maybe he had unfinished business and that was what was keeping him here and he kind of ran from the office."

"He ran? Can ghosts run?" Clove looked intrigued.

"Well, he didn't exactly run, but he floated really quickly."

"Did he say anything?" Thistle looked puzzled.

"He said he didn't have any unfinished business, but even Edith could tell he was lying."

Thistle thought about it a minute. "I bet he's just protecting Brian."

"You just don't like Brian," I interjected.

"You don't like him either," she countered.

"I didn't say I didn't like him. I said I got a weird vibe off him."

"That's the same as saying you don't like him," Thistle argued.

"I think he's nice," Clove offered.

"You think he's hot," Thistle shot back. "There's a difference."

"I don't think he's hot," Clove countered, but her face was reddening under Thistle's increased scrutiny.

"Whatever."

"I don't!"

"Okay, you don't," Thistle said, rolling her eyes in my direction.

"I don't!"

Thistle and I turned our attention away from Clove and back to the store. "Will you guys be done by tonight?" There were still five boxes sitting on the counter waiting to be unpacked.

"We'll be fine," Thistle said. "Once Clove stops thinking about Brian and focuses on her work, that is."

"You're dead to me," Clove grumbled as she returned to the decorations she was sorting.

Thistle and I exchanged knowing looks. Clove had a crush. Of course, the fact that she had a crush on my new boss was a little irritating, but if things worked out, I might be able to eventually work that to my advantage.

What? I was thinking about her well-being. No. I really was.

EIGHT

*A*fter work, I went home long enough to change my clothes and get a notebook so I could cover tonight's bonfire event. It wasn't exactly like it was going to be difficult, but I wanted to make sure we had a good package for Brian's first edition in charge.

When I got home, I found that our living room had been transformed into a big pile of clothes. I figured Clove was underneath some of them, because I could see them moving when I entered the room.

"What's going on?"

Clove looked up from the pile of clothes and regarded me with a stunned look. "It's Thistle. I think she's lost her mind."

"Why do you say that?"

"Just watch."

I sat on the edge of the armchair and waited for whatever travesty Clove had been witnessing. I didn't have to wait long. Thistle flounced out of her bedroom in her bra and underwear and pointed a finger at me accusingly. "I have nothing to wear. I need to go through your closet."

I glanced around at the pile of clothes for a second. "You've tried all these on?"

"Yes."

"Really?"

"Yes."

"You've only been home like twenty minutes and this is like fifty outfits, so that's virtually impossible," I pointed out.

"Most of them she just came out and threw at me and screamed 'how could you let me buy this,'" Clove said helpfully.

"I did not," Thistle scoffed, running her hand through her hair exasperatedly.

I bit the inside of my cheek to keep from laughing out loud. Thistle was clearly on the edge. If I started laughing now, she would cross over to deranged, and then I may be late for the bonfire tonight because Thistle would beat the crap out of me.

"You're nervous," I finally said.

"I am not nervous."

"Yes, you are."

"I am not."

"You are, too."

"This isn't getting us anywhere," Clove interrupted. "What can we do to help?"

"Find me something that doesn't make me look repulsive," Thistle countered.

"None of this makes you look repulsive," Clove said kindly, glancing down at the skirt in her hand. "Although, this skirt does make you look hippy."

"Way to help," I shot back at Clove.

Clove shrugged helplessly.

I blew out a sigh and got to my feet. "Let's approach this one step at a time. First off, we need to settle on an outfit. If Marcus shows up and you're wearing that, he'll pass out before you even leave the house."

Thistle glanced down at her black boyfriend underwear and the matching pushup bra. "You're probably right."

"I know I'm right. Nice to see you put on your fancy underwear just in case, though."

Clove looked scandalized. "You're not planning on sleeping with him on the first date, are you?"

"Of course not," Thistle shot back. "And these are not my fancy underwear."

"Of course they are," I challenged her. "They make your butt look thinner. I have the same pair. I'm not stupid."

Thistle's cheeks flooded with color. "I'm not planning on sleeping with him," she repeated.

"I know," I said encouragingly. "It never hurts to be prepared, though."

"Isn't that the truth," Clove said. "I knew you shaved your legs this morning for a reason."

I sorted through the pile of clothes on the couch for a minute and then turned to Thistle. "I don't think you should wear a skirt," I said honestly.

"Why not?"

"You're going to a bonfire," I pointed out.

"So?"

"You're going to be sitting on bales of hay," I tried again.

"So?"

"So, you don't want straw to poke you in your ... you know ... hoo-ha," Clove supplied.

Thistle and I both swung on Clove. "Her hoo-ha?"

"If you're going to call it that, you're never going to get laid," Thistle grumbled dismissively.

After helping Thistle pick out her most flattering jeans and pairing them with a sparkly tank top and her cutest Madden boots, Clove tackled Thistle's hair while I started applying her makeup.

When we were done, we stepped back to admire our handiwork. She did look fabulous, if I did say so myself.

Thistle regarded herself in the mirror and blew out a sigh. "Do I look okay?"

"You look great," Clove said earnestly.

"You do," I agreed.

Thistle still looked doubtful, but the fight had left her. "Do you think Marcus will like it, though?"

"You really like him," I laughed.

"He's just a guy," Thistle protested.

"If he was just a guy, you wouldn't have changed after work," I pointed out.

"Stop talking to me," Thistle said. "I need to think."

I left Clove to calm Thistle down and changed into a pair of jeans and a flattering V-neck shirt. I grabbed my *Harry Potter* hoodie before leaving the guesthouse. I figured Clove's more even nature would help calm Thistle down before Marcus got there.

When I opened the door, though, I slammed into Marcus' broad chest and found myself rethinking my previous assertion. "Hey," he greeted me in surprise.

"Hi, Marcus," I said a little too loudly. "You're right on time." Promptness is a great trait to possess – except when your date is freaking out thirty feet away.

"I thought that was a good thing?" Marcus looked confused.

"It is," I scrambled to keep him involved in conversation and away from the threshold to the guesthouse.

I could see Thistle and Clove manically gathering all the discarded clothes in the reflection on the front window. I grimaced when I saw them toss the clothes into my room instead of Thistle's. "So, you're going to the bonfire?"

"Yeah. You?"

"I'm on my way there now," I said cheerily.

Marcus narrowed his eyes when he heard something crash in the other room. "What was that?"

"What? I didn't hear anything."

"You didn't hear that big crash? Are you sure everything is okay in there?"

I could see Clove had stumbled over the coffee table and was sprawled on the floor. Thistle was impatiently trying to pull her up off the floor, while simultaneously pinching her on the shoulder to admonish her clumsiness.

"It's fine," I lied.

Marcus waited for a minute, but when he realized I wasn't moving out of the doorway, he furrowed his brow. "Should I leave and come back in a few minutes or something?"

That actually might be helpful. I figured if I told him that, though, he might think we were crazy or something.

"No, I'm ready," I heard Thistle's voice as she stepped up beside me.

Marcus visibly relaxed when he saw Thistle. "You look great," he said. I could tell he meant it.

"Oh, thank you," Thistle said dismissively. "I just threw on the first thing I saw in my closet."

I cast her a sidelong glance but didn't say anything. Thistle may be intent on impressing Marcus, but that wouldn't stop her from wrestling me to the ground and making me eat dirt from the flowerbed if I pissed her off. Then I would really be late.

I stepped aside to let Thistle out, casting a glance back inside to see what Clove was doing. She was rubbing her shoulder where Thistle had pinched her and looking murderous.

I closed the door behind Thistle and started toward my car. "See you at the bonfire."

"Aren't you taking Clove with you?" Thistle asked.

I paused. "I wasn't planning on it."

"Then how is she going to get there?"

I regarded Thistle and Marcus for a second. "I guess I'm waiting for Clove."

Thistle and Marcus headed for his car without a second glance. I walked back into the guesthouse and cast a glance at Clove. "Hurry up."

"Why do I have to hurry?"

"Because if you don't, I'm not giving you a ride and then you won't be able to spy on Marcus and Thistle all night."

Clove met my gaze steadily. "Give me five minutes."

NINE

When we got to the bonfire, I was surprised at how busy the downtown area was. Tourists usually got into the cheesy fun, but this was ridiculous. I ultimately had to park behind the paper and Clove and I walked to the town square.

"You should have just dropped me off," Clove grumbled.

"Why is that?"

"I didn't wear boots with walking in mind."

I glanced down at her spiked heels and couldn't help but agree. "And why did you wear those?"

"They give me three full inches," Clove said proudly.

"That makes you a little more than five feet tall," I pointed out.

"It's better than being four-foot-eleven and a half," she said dismissively.

She had a point.

When we got to the square, Clove headed straight for the hot cider booth. I followed her, even though I didn't like cider. The crowd was thick, and I was worried I would lose her if we separated.

"I can't believe how many people are here," Clove said, sipping on her hot cider.

"I know, it's crazy," I agreed.

"It looks like every inn in the area is booked solid," Clove added, scanning the crowd.

"Yeah. That's good for the town."

"That's good for all of us," Clove agreed.

We lapsed into an amiable silence, happy to just watch the crowd enjoying themselves and listen to the band strumming in the gazebo. I felt Clove stiffen next to me after a few minutes.

"What is it?"

"Brian is here," she exclaimed breathily.

"Great."

Clove ignored my sarcasm. "You should be nice to him. He's going to be your boss for a long time."

"That's not why you want me to be nice to him," I said, snarkiness overtaking my tone.

"He's really handsome, isn't he?"

I followed her gaze and grimaced when I found Brian in the center of the crowd. I couldn't hear what he was saying, but he was clearly trying to schmooze Mrs. Little. I couldn't help but notice that the elderly businesswoman didn't look all that impressed with his charm.

"I guess," I shrugged. "If you like that kind of guy."

"Who wouldn't?"

I looked Brian up and down, taking in his khaki pants and boat shoes, and couldn't hide my shudder. "He's just not my cup of tea."

"So you don't like him at all?" Clove asked. I couldn't help but notice the hopeful tone in her voice. The three of us had made a pact a long time ago that we would never pursue the same guy. We didn't want to end up like our mothers – in more ways than one.

"Not even a little," I promised. "He's all yours."

"I'm not interested in him," Clove said a little too hastily.

"Don't lie," I admonished her. "Oh, look, here he comes."

Brian had caught sight of Clove and me in the crowd and was heading for us with a clear purpose. 'You're here," he said. "I was worried."

"Why were you worried?"

"I didn't want you to miss the story."

"I wouldn't miss the story," I said shortly.

"Hi," Clove greeted him nervously.

"Hi," Brian said, his warm eyes meeting Clove's. I wasn't sure if he actually liked her or if he felt the need to charm everyone he crossed paths with. In truth, I wasn't sure which outcome I was rooting for. I wanted Clove to be happy, but Brian just rubbed me the wrong way.

Brian turned and watched the crowd. I couldn't help but wish he'd go someplace else. I didn't think that was a good sign for our working relationship.

"This is great," Brian said enthusiastically. "I can't believe how many people are here."

"Yeah, it's a great turnout," I echoed hollowly.

"Yeah, a town full of crazies celebrating a murder mystery. Not odd at all."

I froze when I heard the voice. I recognized it instantly. I had spent the better part of the past month trying to forget it. I turned around slowly, trying to refrain from gasping out loud at the sight of the man who was standing behind me.

I would have recognized him anywhere. His shoulder-length black hair was perfect and shiny under the pale lights. His blue eyes were twinkling. His mouth was spread into a wide grin.

"Landon," I greeted him in what I hoped sounded like a normal voice. The last time I had seen him he'd been in a hospital bed after rescuing me and the rest of my family from two crazed murderers and a gang of angry drug dealers.

"Bay," Landon smiled at me uncertainly. He looked like he had been expecting a warmer greeting – like me stripping naked and jumping him in the town square or something.

"Hi, Landon," Clove chirped from my side.

"Hey, Clove," Landon slid a smile in her direction and then turned back to me. "How are things?"

"Things are great," I said with faux brightness. "Things couldn't be better."

"You seem a little tense," Landon pointed out.

"I'm not tense," I lied. The truth was, the emotions that were warring inside of me were more akin to rage and lust. I mentally smacked myself for both of them. This man had no control over my emotions, I reminded myself. None at all.

Landon regarded me seriously. "Fine, you're not tense." He turned to Clove. "What's wrong with her?"

Clove bit her lower lip. "I think she's mad that you didn't call."

I glared at Clove. "I am not," I snapped. "And this is why Thistle thinks you're a blabbermouth."

Clove held up her hands submissively. "I could be making that up," she said lamely.

Landon's eyes twinkled. "Are you making it up? And remember, I'm a duly-sworn officer of the federal government and it's a crime to lie to me."

Clove swallowed hard and shifted her eyes between Landon and me. She clearly felt trapped.

"Don't lie to her," I snapped at Landon.

"I'm not lying. It is a federal crime."

"Only when you're investigating a crime," I replied snottily.

"I am investigating a crime. You stole my heart."

Clove giggled appreciatively. "That was smooth."

"You like that?" Landon asked mischievously.

"I'm sorry, who are you?" Brian had been watching the interaction between the three of us with obvious distaste. I had a feeling that the testosterone was getting ready to fly.

"I'm Landon Michaels," Landon held his hand out to Brian. "And you are?"

Brian took it cautiously. "Brian Kelly. The new owner of The Whistler."

Landon looked Brian up and down. "You're Bay's new boss?"

"Among other things."

Landon narrowed his bright eyes. "What other things?"

Yeah, what things?

"Just things," Brian said evasively.

Landon turned back to me suspiciously. "What things?"

"I have no idea what he's talking about," I said honestly. For the life of me, I couldn't understand why I was explaining myself to the guy who had disappeared from a hospital bed and engaged in silent warfare for the past month.

"Bay's just being coy," Brian said, slinging an arm around my shoulders.

I frowned at him openly, stepping away from him. "No, I'm not."

Landon smiled smugly at Brian. "I think Bay and I need to catch up. You don't mind if I borrow her for a few minutes, do you?"

Landon had phrased it as a question, but the aggressive stance he had taken practically dared Brian to defy him. Brian looked like he was going to argue for a minute and then backed away quickly. "No. Of course not."

Landon grabbed my elbow and guided me a few feet away, not stopping until we were alone in front of Hypnotic. "He seems obnoxious."

"Are you talking about yourself in the third person now?"

Landon grimaced – although it crossed on a smile. His dimples looked like they were coming out to play for a minute, but they quickly disappeared. "Why are you mad at me?"

"I'm not mad," I lied.

"You don't look happy to see me?"

"Why should I?" I challenged him.

"Oh, I don't know, maybe because I saved your life?"

"Oh, please," I sighed. "How long are you going to play that card?"

"It happened a month ago."

"And I haven't seen you in that month," I said bitterly. "I've moved on."

Landon smiled openly now. "Did you miss me?"

Yes. "Not at all."

"I think you're lying," Landon said, reaching out and tweaking a lock of my blonde hair and leaning in uncomfortably close.

I wanted to put some room between us, but I didn't want to seem weak. Instead, I met his gaze solidly. "Why would I lie? I barely know you?"

"That doesn't mean you don't want to see what I look like naked."

I ran my eyes up and down his impressive body for a second. I actually wouldn't mind seeing that. "I can't think of anything more repulsive."

Landon looked at me knowingly. "Give it time. You'll warm up to me again."

I narrowed my eyes suspiciously. "Why?"

"I'm back on the job now. I'll be around a lot more."

"In Hemlock Cove? I doubt it."

"Never say never," he teased me. "Any minute now there could be a brutal murder and my *special talents* could be of some use." His mouth was inches from my ear and I felt myself involuntarily shiver.

I opened my mouth to tell him it would be a cold day in Hell before I would see his special talents up close and personal – or at least a few hours – when a shrill scream punctuated the air.

Landon and I both looked up in surprise when we saw a dark figure stumble into the square. I couldn't be sure in the dark, but I was almost positive it was Ken Trask, the local banker.

Landon moved toward the sound of the disturbance purposely. I was right on his heels.

"What's going on?" He asked when he got to Ken's side.

Up close, I realized that Ken's face was flushed with sweat and he was almost as white as a ghost. "There's a body," he choked out.

"Where?" Landon looked around, his doubt obvious. I think he thought Ken had been partaking in Mrs. Gunderson's 'special' cider. "Isn't the whole point of this week to play murder mystery?"

"That's not supposed to happen until this weekend," I said.

Landon glanced at me, but didn't say anything. He didn't look convinced.

"Where is the body?" I asked Ken.

"Behind the stage," Ken said. "Over by the library."

Landon moved in the direction Ken had pointed. He didn't look back to see if I was following him. I could hear him grumbling as he moved, but I couldn't quite make out what he was saying. I slammed into his back when he pulled up short. "Ow," I muttered, rubbing my nose.

Landon turned back to me gravely. "Find Chief Terry."

"Why?"

"That guy was right. There *is* a body."

I peered around Landon's shoulder. "Are you sure someone didn't just pass out?"

"Not unless they shoved a knife in their own stomach beforehand." Landon's voice was grim.

"What?" I looked toward the direction Landon had been staring and swallowed hard. I didn't know a human body could hold that much blood, let alone spill it on the ground.

Well, shit.

TEN

"Find Chief Terry," Landon repeated. He met my gaze and, for a second, we could both read each other's minds. "And I didn't cause this to happen because of what I said earlier about a murder keeping me in town. I like you, but I don't like you that much."

I moved from Landon's side with the clear purpose of finding Chief Terry but I stopped suddenly. "You like me?"

Landon looked surprised by the question. "Do you really think now is the time to pat yourself on the back?"

"That's not what I was doing," I lied. What? It wasn't.

I swung back around with as much righteous indignation as I could muster and slammed into Chief Terry. "What the hell?" I sputtered. I wasn't exactly exuding gracefulness this evening.

"What's going on?" Chief Terry's voice had taken on a hard edge. He had grabbed my shoulders to steady me, but was peering around me in Landon's direction.

"There's a body," I pointed toward Landon, rubbing my nose ruefully.

I noticed that the entire town had stopped celebrating and was now moving in our direction. Chief Terry followed my gaze. "Shit," he grumbled. "This is the last thing we need."

"They probably think it is part of the murder mystery," I pointed out.

"Of course they do." Chief Terry looked nonplussed. He saw one of his deputies join the fray at the edge of the crowd.

"Duncan, get the names of everyone here," he ordered. "Then get them out of here. We don't need them contaminating the crime scene."

Deputy Duncan nodded and quickly turned back to the crowd. "Everyone, please line up and identify yourself to me or one of the other officers and then return to your home or wherever you're staying tonight."

Mrs. Little broke in. "This was just some unfortunate accident," she soothed the obviously frazzled crowd. "What's a murder mystery without an actual murder?"

"Good grief," Landon muttered. "This whole town is like a psych experiment."

Mrs. Little rounded on Landon angrily. "What did you just say?"

"I said this whole town is like a psych experiment," Landon repeated arrogantly.

"And who are you?"

Landon pulled his badge out of his pocket and flashed it at Mrs. Little derisively. "I'm a federal agent."

"And that gives you the right to be an *ass?*"

I smirked in Landon's direction. Mrs. Little was mean to everyone – she didn't care if they had a badge or not.

"Mrs. Little, we need to clear the scene," Chief Terry said gently. I could tell he was worried Mrs. Little would cause a scene.

"We don't want to panic the tourists," I said helpfully. I hoped that would be enough to distract her.

Mrs. Little must have realized the wisdom of my statement, because she returned to her crowd control endeavors. "This is just an unfortunate event," she told everyone as the assembled officers herded them back toward the town square. "Everything is perfectly fine. It's probably just some kind of sick joke."

When she was gone, Landon spoke again. "She's a trip."

He had no idea.

Chief Terry pulled up straighter and took a step toward Landon. "Agent Michaels. What brings you to our small town?" Chief Terry didn't seem especially thrilled by Landon's presence.

"I was just catching up with an old friend," Landon said, shooting a glance in my direction.

Chief Terry's gaze darkened as he looked down at me. "I thought I told you to stay away from this guy?"

"That was when he was undercover as a drug dealer. I didn't know it was a blanket statement that encompassed forever."

Chief Terry harrumphed and then carefully stepped over to Landon's side. "Are you sure he's dead?"

"Yeah. No one could survive losing that much blood."

I made a move to join Landon and Chief Terry, but Chief Terry raised his hand to stop me. "I don't want you stepping on the evidence."

"You and Landon are stepping on the evidence."

"We're trained to step on the evidence."

Whatever.

I watched Chief Terry and Landon circle the body for a few minutes. Curiosity got the better of my common sense. "Who is it?"

"Myron Grisham," Chief Terry answered without thinking.

"You're kidding?"

"Nope."

Every town has a town drunk. Myron Grisham was Hemlock Cove's. Despite his substance abuse problem, he was mostly harmless. The town took turns feeding him and housing him – when he would let them – all in an effort to keep him from passing out all across town.

While most drunks had a mean side, Myron was mainly a danger to himself. I had never heard of him threatening anyone – or anyone threatening him -- for that matter. Basically, he had come back from

Desert Storm fifteen years ago with memories bad enough that they drove him to drink – and the town was sympathetic to his plight.

"And he was stabbed?"

Chief Terry looked at me incredulously. "Do you not see the knife?"

"Don't get snippy with me," I charged. "I was just asking a question."

"I wasn't getting snippy."

"Aunt Tillie would think you were being snippy," I shot back.

Chief Terry openly blanched. "Don't you tell her I was being snippy with you, I can't deal with that woman's wrath *and* a murder."

That was too much for any mortal man, I silently agreed. I felt a presence move in beside me. I didn't have to look down to know it was Clove. "It's Myron Grisham."

"You're kidding," Clove's eyes nearly shot off her forehead. "How did he die?"

"I'm betting that big knife in his stomach had something to do with it." Great. She'd brought Brian with her.

"Nice observation."

Brian ignored my sarcasm. "I guess we have a bigger story than the murder mystery this week," he said excitedly.

I glared at him. "You seem happy about that."

"I'm not happy a man is dead," Brian looked properly chastised. "But we'll definitely sell more copies of the paper with a murder on the front page."

And *that's* what really mattered.

Chief Terry focused on Brian for the first time since his arrival. "You're the new owner of the paper?"

"Yes," Brian said proudly.

"Well, don't be an ass."

Brian's smile faded. "I didn't mean to .... "

"Why don't you just go over there and let the professionals do their job?" Landon suggested.

"Fine," Brian said stiffly. He turned to me and pasted a fake chivalrous look on his face. "Can I escort you ladies back home?"

AMANDA M. LEE

I saw Landon get to his feet with clear irritation. I decided to head off the situation. "We'll be fine," I said smoothly.

"There's a killer out there," Brian said pragmatically, sliding a smug glance in Landon's direction. "You need someone to protect you."

Chief Terry placed his hands on his hips. He looked as irritated as Landon. "They'll be fine," he said. "Besides, they have Aunt Tillie. There's no murderer in the world who can stand up to that woman."

I glanced at Chief Terry and Landon, genuinely torn. I wanted to know what had happened, but I knew that neither one of them was going to let me in on the investigation – especially with Brian around.

"You'll call me tomorrow?" I asked Chief Terry.

"Yeah," he said tiredly, running his hands through his gray hair. "I'll call you tomorrow."

I nodded silently and started to move with Clove back toward the town square. I wasn't surprised to see that almost everyone had fled the vicinity since Ken's announcement that he'd found a body – a real body that had nothing to do with the murder mystery.

I cast one glance back in Landon's direction. His features were unreadable. I then fell into step with Clove and headed toward my car. Brian followed meekly behind us. "Why is he scared of your Aunt Tillie?"

"You've met her."

"Yeah, but she's an old woman."

"Why don't you tell her that the next time you see her," I suggested.

ELEVEN

I didn't sleep very well that night. Go figure.

My dreams were a jumble of blood, ghosts, and dead bodies. The fact that Landon slipped in shirtless didn't escape me – but I did choose to ignore that little tidbit, for the time being at least. My mind can only handle so much optical stimulation at one time.

When I finally decided to embrace consciousness, I slowly climbed out of bed and started to drag myself to the living room. Since I wasn't watching where I was going, and my eyes were only half open, I stumbled on the huge pile of clothes Thistle and Clove had hidden in my bedroom the night before and slammed into my bedroom door as I lost my footing.

"Mother ...!"

Clove opened the door and regarded me sprawled on the floor speculatively. "Don't finish that sentence. Aunt Tillie can hear you curse from miles away."

I rubbed my ankle morosely from my position on the floor and regarded Clove with abject irritation. "Why did you guys dump all these clothes in my room?"

"It was closer," Clove shrugged.

I regained my footing, sweeping up the majority of Thistle's discarded wardrobe in one swoop, and dramatically stalked out of the bedroom. I strode across the living room, threw open Thistle's bedroom door, and tossed all of her clothes onto her bed. "I'm returning your stuff!"

By the time I realized she wasn't alone, it was too late. Thistle and Marcus were intertwined on the bed. And while the sheets covered everything I didn't want to see, it was obvious they were both naked. *Crud.*

"What the hell!" Thistle's eyes shot open. Marcus was awake, but he was still getting his bearings. "Don't you knock?"

Clove had followed me into the bedroom and was staring at the scene in front of us with her mouth agape. "No way! You slept with him!"

"Say it a little louder, Clove," Thistle grumbled. "I don't think Aunt Tillie can hear you from here."

"Don't be so sure," I mumbled.

Marcus had realized where he was and was fruitlessly trying to hide under the covers. I could see why Thistle was so enamored with him. He was ripped. All that stall cleaning obviously paid off in the muscles department.

"Stop staring," Thistle ordered. "Get out."

Clove was still distracted by Marcus' bronzed skin and rippling muscles so I dragged her out behind me and shut the door. I tasked Clove with making coffee and turned on the television to see if last night's murder had made the news yet. It hadn't.

"How can they not have the story yet?" Clove asked.

"It was late when it happened, and the only people there were townspeople and tourists. It will make the news by tonight, for sure," I replied.

"Are you going to call Chief Terry?"

"I'll just stop in at the department on my way into work."

Clove brewed a pot of coffee and slid the first cup toward me. She tossed a few slices of bread into the toaster for breakfast, and then sat down next to me to eat them. "Who do you think would kill Myron?"

"I don't know," I sipped my coffee and shrugged.

"Someone killed Myron?"

Clove and I looked up to see Thistle and Marcus walking into the room. Neither one of us had heard the door open, so we were surprised by their sudden appearance. Sadly, Marcus was completely dressed.

"You didn't know that?"

"No. When?" Thistle directed Marcus toward the stool on my left and poured two cups of coffee. She slid one across the counter toward Marcus and then fixed a hard gaze on me. "Why didn't you tell me?"

"I assumed you knew," I replied. Marcus' presence – even though he was now fully clothed – was something of a distraction. "It happened at the bonfire last night. You were there."

"We never actually made it," Thistle shifted uncomfortably.

"Really?" I smiled slyly in Thistle's direction. "Where did you go?"

"We went for a moonlight horse ride, if you must know," Thistle shot back. I heard her grumble "busybody" under her breath.

"There's nothing like the smell of horse crap in the moonlight to entice you to drop your panties," I smirked.

If Marcus were any redder, he'd spontaneously combust. "I should get to work," he said uncomfortably.

"Don't let Bay chase you off," Clove chided me. "We're teasing Thistle, not you."

"It's not that," Marcus lied. "I just have to get back to work."

Clove and I wisely held our tongues as we watched Thistle walk Marcus to the door and say goodbye. When she came back to the kitchen, she didn't look happy. "Both of you are dead to me. You're such ... witches."

"How were we supposed to know that you brought him home," I complained. "We never saw you last night and we just assumed you came home after us. We didn't realize you were already home – and otherwise engaged – before we got here." I sipped my coffee and watched Thistle carefully. She looked pissed.

"You love this, don't you?"

"I don't hate it," I admitted.

Thistle narrowed her eyes as she regarded me. "If I were you, I'd forget what you saw."

"I don't think I can do that," I said carefully. "It's not that often that you see a washboard on a man and not at the river or in a museum."

Clove giggled appreciatively.

"I can't wait until your mom finds out you had sex on the first date."

That did it. Thistle practically flew over the counter and tackled me backwards. We both hit the ground hard. I could feel her tugging my hair as she tried to pin me to the ground. "You're not telling anyone about this," she seethed.

Thistle had taken me by surprise, and she had the leverage. I couldn't manage to buck her off me, no matter how hard I tried. "I can't breathe," I complained.

"Promise you're not going to say anything," Thistle growled.

"I won't say anything," I promised. I couldn't guarantee the aunts wouldn't find out some other way, though. It was eerie how they managed to know things we went out of our way to lie to them about.

Thistle had managed to successfully pin me to the ground – and she didn't look like she was going to get off my chest anytime soon. "I'm not joking," she warned me.

"I won't tell," I grunted, shifting my midriff so she tumbled off to the side. I knew I wouldn't be able to do it if she didn't let me.

We both got up and returned to our cups of coffee silently. After a few minutes, Thistle broke the silence. "So Myron is really dead?"

"Yeah, someone stabbed him behind the town square, right next to the library, and left his body out in the open."

Clove was still nervous as she watched us for signs we were going to tussle again. "There was a lot of blood," she said warily.

"Are you sure it wasn't just a fake out for the murder mystery weekend?" Thistle asked.

"Not according to Chief Terry and Landon," I said dismissively.

"Landon?" Thistle looked surprised.

"Yeah, he showed up last night – right before another body dropped in town."

"Why was he here?" Thistle asked.

"I don't know," I shrugged.

"He came to see Bay," Clove supplied.

"He did not," I scoffed.

"He came to see Bay?" Thistle turned to Clove. She had an evil look on her face.

"It was pretty obvious," Clove said. "He even got all puffed out when Brian showed up. He was marking his territory like a dog."

"Well, that's interesting," Thistle mused, casting an appraising look in my direction. Crap. Now she had dirt on me.

"He was not here because of me," I countered.

"Then why was he here?"

"I have no idea."

"How did he look?"

"Hot," Clove interjected immediately.

Thistle turned back to me. "He is pretty good looking."

"He's okay," I hedged.

"Do you think he's sticking around for the investigation into Myron's death?"

That thought hadn't even occurred to me. "I have no idea."

"I bet he gets himself assigned to the case," Thistle said mischievously.

"I wonder how long it will be before Landon takes Bay for a twilight ride," Clove giggled.

I stood up determinedly. "I have to get ready for work."

I could hear Thistle and Clove betting how long it would take for Landon to separate me from my panties as I left the room. Clove was betting on a week and Thistle was betting on three days.

Even I was curious which one of them would be right.

TWELVE

*W*hen I left the guesthouse, Clove and Thistle were whispering conspiratorially at the counter in the kitchen. I didn't bother telling them goodbye. I figured I would see them in a couple of hours for lunch – and by then, Thistle would hopefully be markedly calmer.

I stopped at the police department on my way to The Whistler, pulling in behind the department and quickly exiting my car. It was still early, most of the town hadn't come to life yet, but I didn't want to risk running into anyone before I knew exactly what was going on.

The Hemlock Cove Police Department is small, only a couple of rooms and a small reception area. I greeted Greta, the office secretary, when I entered the office. She was used to my visits so she didn't even try to stop me when I wandered into the back hallway that led to Chief Terry's office.

I navigated the narrow hall and opened Chief Terry's office door without knocking. I figured he would be expecting me.

I pulled up short when I found Landon sitting in one of the chairs across from Chief Terry's desk. He seemed surprised to see me in the doorway. "Don't you knock?"

"I didn't know you were in here," I said sheepishly. I couldn't help but notice that Landon didn't look like he'd been home – or gotten any sleep. He was dressed in the same clothes he'd been wearing the night before and he had pronounced dark circles under his eyes.

""You just let her wander in here?" Landon was talking to Chief Terry, but he was looking at me.

"She doesn't do well with the word no," Chief Terry said tiredly. "No one in her family does."

"I don't doubt that," Landon grumbled.

I ignored Landon's obvious sarcasm and sat down in the other chair. I turned to Chief Terry expectantly. "So what do we know?"

"We know that you aren't a part of this investigation," Landon interjected shortly.

"No one is talking to you," I shot back. "Do we have any idea who stabbed Myron?"

"He's not going to answer that," Landon said.

"We don't know who," Chief Terry said. "The autopsy is being performed in about an hour. We'll know more then."

"Why are you telling her that?" Landon looked perplexed.

"Why not?"

"She's a reporter," Landon pointed out.

"She's a reporter for a weekly," Chief Terry shot back. "Even if she wanted to print something about the murder, the paper doesn't come out for days. Calm down."

Landon looked flabbergasted. "So you just tell her whatever she wants to know?"

Chief Terry shrugged. "I guess so."

"Well, now that I'm the lead on this case, I'm going to have to ask you not to share information with the press," Landon said smartly.

"You're the lead on the case?"

"That surprises you?" Landon raised his eyebrows in my direction. I was starting to rethink his ability to separate me from my panties on the spot. His dismissive attitude didn't exactly endear him to me.

"I don't understand why you're even involved," I countered.

"I'm an FBI agent."

"And this is a local issue. And, as you can see, we have a local police chief who is perfectly capable of conducting an investigation all by himself," I said, gesturing to Chief Terry. "You don't need help, do you?"

"I ..."

"Who are you to tell him he doesn't need help?" Landon charged back. "When did you become an expert in crime solving?"

"I'm not an expert," I replied. "But Chief Terry is. We don't need you."

"Obviously you do. Besides, I was the first one on the scene, and that's always an edge when it comes to solving a crime."

"You were on the scene for like thirty seconds before Chief Terry," I argued.

"Hey! Before is before."

"If you two are done verbally copulating, we have a dead man to investigate," Chief Terry interjected irritably.

I glared in Chief Terry's direction. "Oh, now you're on his side?"

"I'm not on anyone's side, especially not his," Chief Terry said. "I don't have a lot of choice in the matter. "

I opened my mouth to argue further, but Chief Terry held up his hand to stop me. "We have twice the number of people in this town than we usually have, and I'm going to need help. I'm not ashamed to admit it."

I couldn't hide my frown, even though I could see where Chief Terry was coming from. This was going to make my job so much harder than usual. I didn't want to have to go to Landon for information. That would give him leverage – and I wasn't sure I wanted him having leverage over me at this point in time.

"It was obviously someone with ties to the town," I offered.

"How do you figure?" Landon asked.

"Why would a stranger want to kill the town drunk?"

"Why would someone from the town want to kill him?" Landon countered.

"At least he has ties to the people in the town," I argued. "The town works overtime to keep him away from the tourists."

"You know a lot about Myron Grisham. Maybe we should consider you a suspect?" Landon's suggestion was biting.

"Maybe we should. Or maybe we should consider you a suspect?"

"Excuse me?"

"The last time we had a dead body you were knee deep in it. The minute you come back to town we have another dead body. Coincidence? I don't think so."

"Hey, you were knee deep in the last dead body, too," Landon pointed out. "And you brought your entire family to a cornfield in the middle of the night, for some reason. You still haven't explained that, by the way."

I turned to Chief Terry for help, but his head was buried in his hands and he was rubbing his scalp like he had a killer migraine. I didn't blame him. Landon and I were taking immaturity to a whole new level. "Aren't you going to say anything?"

"I'm not really interested in playing psychologist for the two of you right now," Chief Terry replied. "I don't think I'm qualified."

I rolled my eyes in Chief Terry's direction. "I can't believe you're not standing up for me. Or my family. My mom and aunts are going to be so disappointed." Dirty, I know. I'm not above pulling the family card, though.

"You wouldn't," Chief Terry warned.

"If you try to keep me out of this case, I most definitely would," I shot back. "No warm dinners for you in the immediate future, I can promise that."

Chief Terry sighed. "We won't keep you out of the case."

"We won't?" Landon looked stunned. "Why? Because she threatened to tell her mommy?"

"She could provide valuable help," Chief Terry said. "And don't say anything negative about her mother."

"How?"

"She's just ... very, very good at what she does," Chief Terry replied.

Chief Terry was well aware of the rumors that floated around town about my family. He had never come right out and asked me if we had special abilities, but he had taken me to a crime scene or two. I think he knew that there was something different about me – and Clove and Thistle, for that matter – but he either didn't want to know or was scared to know what that 'something special' was.

I shot Landon a victorious smile and got to my feet. "I'll check in this afternoon after you get the autopsy results."

With those words, I flounced out of the office without a backwards glance.

"I can't wait," Landon grumbled.

THIRTEEN

*A*fter leaving the police department, I went to The Whistler to do some research. Edith and William were waiting in my office for me – and the parking lot was empty – so I figured Brian hadn't made it into work yet.

"What's up?"

"We heard that Myron was killed last night," William said. If a ghost could look pale – paler than usual, that is -- I would think that William was about to pass out. He looked shaken, for lack of a better word.

"Yeah, he was found behind the town square with a knife sticking out of his stomach," I said. "Right by the library."

"Do they know who did it?" Edith had been a ghost for decades. I didn't think she had any idea who Myron was, but she did like to gossip with the best of them.

"Not yet," I said.

"They didn't see anyone around?" William asked.

"No."

"How do they know it wasn't an accident? Or suicide?"

"I don't know anyone who accidentally shoves a huge hunting

knife in their own stomach, or chooses that way to commit suicide. There's got to be a better way to go than that."

"That's horrible," William shuddered a heavy sigh.

I turned to William, my curiosity evident. "Did you know Myron well?"

William looked uncomfortable. "Of course, I knew him. Everyone in town knew him. He was a good boy before he went off to that war and it ruined him."

That made sense, but there was something weird about William's reaction to Myron's death. I just couldn't decide why he cared so much. I wracked my brain for memories of William and Myron together. All I could come up with, though, was William giving Myron a place to sleep a handful of times. Given the fact that Myron was usually drunk, that statement could be applied to any number of the town's denizens on a regular basis.

"It's sad," I said finally. "I didn't know Myron well. He just seemed like a really sad guy."

"He was sad," William said.

I wanted to question William further, but I heard the front door of the office open. I wasn't surprised to see Brian at my open office door within a minute. "So, what did you find out about the dead guy?"

"His name was Myron," William growled at his oblivious grandson.

"They're not doing the autopsy on Myron until sometime this morning," I said, trying not to stare at William to see his reaction. "We'll know more this afternoon."

Brian looked disappointed. "Does it usually take this long to do an autopsy?"

"We share a coroner with three other towns," I explained.

"Why?"

"We don't have enough suspicious deaths to warrant keeping our own on the payroll."

"That makes sense," Brian said finally. He still looked a little disappointed – which bugged the crap out of me.

I looked up at him expectantly. "Is there something else I can help you with?"

"Huh?" Brian clearly had trouble with knowing when he wasn't wanted. "Oh, no. Go back to work. I'll be in my office fixing things up if you need me."

Once Brian left, I Googled Myron on my laptop. I wasn't surprised with what I came up with. There were a few articles about his track prowess from his high school days – and even an article about him returning to Hemlock Cove after the war. After that, though, there was nothing.

Even though Myron had been something of an embarrassment for the town, he had never been arrested and didn't have a criminal record. Since he was technically homeless, I had once heard he had a small shack out by the Black Creek – a small tributary of the Hollow Creek -- but I had never seen it. There weren't any property records either. He obviously didn't have a Facebook or Twitter account.

After a couple hours of fruitless searching, I left the office and made my way down to Hypnotic. Clove and Thistle were busy helping customers when I entered, so I kept silent while I waited for them to finish up.

Clove could read minds – or rather she could read auras and sense what people were feeling – so she was the resident 'psychic.' Basically, she read tarot cards and told visitors what they wanted to hear. She was busy helping a young couple now – and they couldn't help marveling at the wonder of her insight.

"I am a total nurturer," the young woman gushed. "You're amazing."

Thistle was behind the counter helping a woman load up on homemade candles and power crystals. After about twenty minutes, it was just the three of us in the store.

"Did you find out anything about Myron?" Thistle asked.

"Not much. They won't have the autopsy results until this afternoon at the earliest. More likely tomorrow morning," I replied.

"Did Chief Terry tell you anything else?"

"He's not in charge of the case," I said.

"He's not? Who is? The state police?" Clove looked angry. None of us liked it when the state came in to take over an investigation. We were all loyal to Chief Terry – even if I did threaten to cut off his food supply.

"No, Landon," I said bitterly.

Thistle smirked. "He took over the case? Why?"

"Because he wants to torture me."

"Or because he wants a reason to be in town and stay near you." Clove has a romantic streak that borders on sweet – or annoying.

"I doubt that's it."

"Really? Because he's heading this way."

I looked up to see Thistle gazing out of the window at the front of the store. I refused to look. "Very funny."

"I'm not joking."

"You're just trying to get back at me for this morning."

I heard the front door of the store open; marked by the wind chimes they had strategically placed there, and felt my stomach drop to my feet. There was no way she was telling the truth. Was there?

I kept telling myself not to give her the satisfaction of turning around, and yet I couldn't stop myself from doing just that. It was a like a power that was bigger than me had suddenly taken control of my body

"I figured I'd find you here," Landon greeted me. He walked around the side of the couch and plopped down next to me. "I'm assuming you were telling your cousins about this morning."

"We were deciding what we were going to have for lunch," I lied.

Landon didn't look like he believed me, but he let it go. "Great. I'm starved."

I grimaced. "No one invited you to lunch," I pointed out.

"Do you like Middle Eastern?" Thistle asked, shooting me a triumphant look. This was her payback. I was going to make her eat a whole mud pie later, I swear.

"I love Middle Eastern," Landon said warmly. "Can you order me a chicken shawarma and fattoush salad?"

"Sure," Thistle said, turning to me. "You want your usual?"

"Yes," I grumbled.

Landon waited for Thistle to place the order and join the rest of us before he started talking again. "So, what can you guys tell me about Myron Grisham?"

"Don't help him," I warned Thistle and Clove. "He's out to get Chief Terry. Don't forget that."

If Thistle and Clove were anxious to help Landon initially, my warning reminded them of their loyalty to Chief Terry. They both snapped their mouths shut grimly.

Landon shot me a disgusted look. "Nice. I'm not out to get Chief Terry," Landon explained simply. "I'm helping Chief Terry. He's the one who explained just that to Bay this morning."

Thistle looked me up and down. "Is that true?"

"Who are you going to believe?"

"You answered a question with a question," Clove pointed out. "You always said that was a sign that someone was lying."

I glared at Clove pointedly. She pretended she didn't notice. "What do you want to know?"

"What have you got?"

"Not much," Thistle admitted.

"I thought everyone in this town knew everything about everyone else?"

"That's true, but Myron was ... Myron was different," Clove finished lamely.

"How?"

"He was like a local track hero in high school," Thistle started. "That was before we were born. He was kind of a local celebrity, though. He was the only athlete we ever had who qualified for the state playoffs in anything."

Landon listened quietly. I couldn't help but notice that he didn't interrupt Thistle like he regularly interrupted me.

"He went to college on some sort of scholarship," Thistle continued. "He was gone for like five years and then he came back to town for a couple of years. I have no idea what he did during that time. I think he owned a business or something, but I'm not really sure."

"Chief Terry said he owned a restaurant," Landon interjected.

"Really?" Thistle seemed surprised. "I can't imagine letting him around food, but okay, I believe you."

"What else?"

"He joined the Army after that. He was in Desert Storm. When he came back, he started drinking and he never really stopped."

"Desert Storm?" Landon looked surprised. "Wasn't he in his late fifties?"

"Yeah," Clove looked nonplussed. "I think he went to school with my mom and our aunts."

"Well, that would have made him in his thirties during Desert Storm," Landon pointed out.

"So?"

"It's just that most people don't join the Army when they're in their thirties," Landon said.

Huh, I had never really thought about that. "So why would he join the Army in his thirties?"

"I have no idea," Landon shrugged.

Thistle was chewing her lip when I looked up. I knew that meant she had remembered something, but she was trying to decide if she should say it in front of Landon.

"What?"

"It's just ... ." Thistle broke off.

"What?"

"I think he used to date Marnie," she said finally.

"Now that you mention it, I think you're right," I admitted.

"Who is Marnie?" Landon looked confused.

"My mom," Clove answered.

"Your mom used to date the deceased?"

"Not recently," Clove explained. "I think it was before he went off to the war."

"You're saying your mom drove a man to enlist in the Army?" Landon was going for levity; I couldn't help but feel annoyed at his comment, though.

"I don't think it was that," I challenged Landon. Even as I said the

74

words, though, I couldn't be sure that they were true. One look at Thistle and Clove and I could tell they were thinking the same thing. The women in our family were known to drive men to insanity. This wouldn't be the first time.

Landon didn't seem to notice our distraction. "I guess I need to talk to Marnie."

Good luck with that.

"Why don't you come to dinner tonight," Thistle offered. "I'm sure she'd be happy to talk to you. And all the aunts will want to see you after you saved our lives. You're like a family hero."

If I could mentally choke someone, like a dark Jedi Knight, Thistle would be dead on the floor.

"I can't wait," Landon said enthusiastically, shooting me a flirty smile.

He'd change his mind on that front pretty quickly, I figured. Aunt Tillie would make sure of it.

FOURTEEN

$\mathcal{T}$he rest of lunch was a casual affair. Landon started grilling Thistle and Clove on what I was like as a child. As much as Thistle wanted to mess with me, though, she wasn't about to start spilling family secrets.

The truth was, I was an odd child – even for my family's standards. I could talk to ghosts at a young age. Everyone in town, though, thought I wandered around talking to myself. As close as Thistle and Clove and I were, even they didn't understand what I was doing when I was holding entire conversations with shrubs and flowers. It took a long time for me to realize what was going on, and even more time for me to explain what was going on to Clove and Thistle.

My cousins remained friendly with Landon, despite his probing questions, but they didn't reveal anything to him that would put the family secret in jeopardy. If Landon suspected anything, he didn't let on.

Once he was gone, with a promise that he would be up at the inn at 7 p.m. sharp, I turned on Thistle. "Why did you invite him to dinner?"

"You know why," Thistle said dismissively.

"You've paid me back for the Marcus thing this morning," I complained. "Good grief."

"That's just an added bonus," Thistle said. "I invited him because you like him and you're not going to make the first move."

"That's not why you invited him," I countered.

"It is so."

"It is not."

"It is so."

"It is not." .

"It is so."

"I'm going to grind your face into the mud when this is all over," I promised. "You better not have any dessert."

I returned to the office, but I didn't get much done. I called Chief Terry, but he said the autopsy results wouldn't be available until the next morning. I was worried that would be the case. Finally, I packed up my laptop and went home.

Clove and Thistle were already at the guesthouse when I arrived. They were watching me expectantly.

"What?"

"What are you going to wear?" Clove asked.

I looked down at my jeans and simple tee and shrugged. "This."

"You can't wear that," Clove waved me off. "He's already seen you in that. Don't you want to dress up?"

"No. This isn't a date."

Clove and Thistle exchanged knowing looks, but dropped the matter. A few minutes before seven, we all left for the inn on foot. There was no sense in driving, even though the nights were getting markedly cooler on a daily basis.

We let ourselves in through the back door, ignoring Aunt Tillie who was sitting in her chair watching *Jeopardy*, and headed straight into the kitchen. I wanted to give Marnie a heads up about Landon before he arrived for dinner.

The minute we entered the kitchen, though, the rich scent of homemade lasagna assaulted my nasal passages. Lasagna was one of my favorite dishes. My mouth was actually salivating at the smell.

"Lasagna?"

"It's your favorite," my mom said warmly. "We heard you found another dead body last night and figured you could use some comfort food."

"That's nice," I said, and I meant it.

"Of course, we should have served liver," my mom sad.

Blech. I hated liver. "Why should you have served liver?"

"Well, since we had to hear about you finding another body from Chief Terry, you don't exactly deserve to be rewarded, do you?" My mother was giving me her patented 'I'm disappointed in you' look.

Crap.

"I didn't think it was a big deal," I lied.

"Oh, please," Marnie scoffed from her place at the counter. She was busy icing a fancy looking carrot cake. If they were really fixing my favorite meals it would have been a red velvet cake. I suddenly didn't feel so guilty about not telling them about the dead body.

"Oh, please, what?"

"You three lie about everything, whether it's a good idea or not. You've done it since you were kids."

"That's not true," Clove protested.

"Really?" Marnie challenged her. "The first time you were felt up you came home with your sweater on backwards and raced upstairs to tell these two," she gestured at Thistle and me. "Then the three of you came downstairs and when I asked you about it, you said that the wind must have shifted the sweater."

"You knew?" Clove looked horrified.

"Little Donnie Bailey. His dad had wandering hands, too."

Thistle barked out a laugh. It was always funny when their wrath was directed at someone else.

"What are you laughing at," Twila interrupted. "You were the one who lied about finding lipstick on the sidewalk when you were really stealing it."

Thistle swallowed hard. "I did not steal it."

"You were caught on camera, and I had to go in and pay for it," Twila pointed out.

"It only happened once." Thistle was suddenly obsessed with her shoes.

"It did," I backed up Thistle loyally.

She shot me a grateful look.

"And none of you told us about the overnight guest you had last night," my mom interjected. "Marcus is a handsome boy, though."

Uh-oh.

Thistle shot me a venomous look. "It wasn't me," I protested.

"We saw him slinking off this morning," Aunt Tillie said, entering the room dramatically. I couldn't help but notice she was still wearing her sunglasses.

"He wasn't slinking off," Thistle argued.

"And I suppose he was there to fix the plumbing," Aunt Tillie said haughtily.

Well, he did clear out Thistle's pipes. "What does it matter?" I challenged.

"It doesn't," my mom chided me. "It's just another example of the continuous stream of lies the three of you spew."

"We don't lie," Clove disputed my mom. One look at her warning glare and Clove shrank in her growing countenance. "We don't lie all the time," she amended.

We so need to change the subject. "You guys remember the FBI agent from the cornfield?"

My mom looked surprised by the change in subject matter. "The one who saved our lives? The one with all the pretty dark hair?"

That would be the one. "Yeah, Landon Michaels. He's investigating Myron's death."

"Why isn't Terry investigating it?" Twila asked.

"They're investigating it together," I said. "Anyway, he's coming to dinner tonight."

"Are you dating?" My mom looked far too excited by the prospect.

"No," I said hurriedly.

"Then why is he coming to dinner?"

"He wants to talk to Marnie," Thistle said.

"Why?" Marnie looked surprised.

"We might have told him that you used to date Myron, you know, back in the day," Thistle said lamely, dropping her gaze in an attempt to avoid the fire bolts that were shooting from Marnie.

"And why would you tell him that?"

"He asked," Clove supplied.

"So, let me get this straight," Marnie was practically seething. "You three lie about minor things and then decide to tell the truth about something like this?"

"We didn't think it would be a big deal," I said. *Why was it such a big deal?*

"It's not a big deal," Marnie waved me off. "It just never ceases to amaze me what you guys tell the truth about and what you lie about."

"They're just not very smart," Aunt Tillie interjected.

"Excuse me? You're wearing sunglasses in the house because you believe you're allergic to oxygen and we're the stupid ones?" The minute I said the words, I knew it was a mistake.

Aunt Tillie shuffled toward me. I wasn't tall at five-five, but I towered over Aunt Tillie in physical stature. Somehow, though, I felt dwarfed by her presence. Aunt Tillie extended one gnarled finger in my direction. "You should be careful who you call stupid, my dear. Karma is a bitch. And yours is starting to show."

What the hell did that mean?

Aunt Tillie turned away dismissively. "If you were bringing a date, you really should have cleaned yourself up."

"It's not a date."

"There are great home electrolysis systems these days," she said as she started to move toward the dining room. "You really should invest in one."

If Karma is real, why is Aunt Tillie still standing?

FIFTEEN

*A*fter a quick trip to the bathroom, where I found Aunt Tillie's mustache had suddenly re-grown, I returned to the kitchen.

"It's hardly noticeable, dear," my mom patted my arm.

It better not be, I'd used her razor to get rid of it. After my mom and aunts took the food out to the kitchen, I turned to Thistle. "Whatever you're planning for that old lady, I'm in."

"She really is the Devil," Thistle lamented. I noticed that she was running her own hand over her own top lip to make sure her mustache hadn't returned. None of us felt safe.

Clove licked her lips nervously. "If we do something to her, it will just make her mad." I couldn't help but notice that she was looking around the room like Aunt Tillie would jump out from behind a curtain to pounce at the hint of a plot against her. Actually, that wasn't entirely out of the realm of possibility.

"We can't just let her go unchecked," Thistle hissed. "It makes her feel omnipotent – which really just makes her more dangerous."

"Are you sure she's not?"

"What? Omnipotent? No one is omnipotent."

The three of us lapsed into an uneasy silence. Even we weren't sure that was true when it came to Aunt Tillie.

We all collected ourselves, shaking off the shudder that had suddenly overwhelmed us, and followed our mothers into the dining room. I noticed that Landon was already seated, and Brian was located a few chairs down. They were both shooting each other dark looks.

"What took you so long?" My mom asked.

"We were just ... it was like thirty seconds," I grumbled.

"Well, when the three of you are together plotting, things can fall apart in thirty seconds," my mom clucked. "I was just checking."

Just checking, my ass!

Thistle and Clove hurriedly slid into seats on Aunt Tillie's side of the table, leaving the only open chair situated next to Landon. I glared at both of them, but silently sat down next to him. I didn't bother greeting him, mostly because I felt like everyone at the table was staring at me. Damn Aunt Tillie.

After dinner had been doled out, most of the guests at the far end of the table were talking amongst themselves. That left our end of the table mired in an uncomfortable silence. My mom, apparently, couldn't stand it.

"It's so nice to see you," she said to Landon.

"You, too," Landon replied amiably.

My mom smiled when she caught sight of his dimples. Who didn't love dimples? "I see you still have long hair," she hedged. She obviously didn't love that.

"I like it long," Landon said with a smile, although I could tell the smile was tighter than it should have been.

"What does your mom think about your hair?"

Thistle exchanged a humorous smile with me. We were enjoying Landon's discomfort.

"She doesn't like it," Landon said honestly. "I'm an adult, though. I just tell her that parents lose the right to comment on their child's hair after the age of eighteen."

Twila shuffled a look toward Thistle's hair. I could tell she thought differently.

"So, where have you been?" Aunt Tillie threw out the question ominously. Apparently Landon's dimples didn't charm her.

Landon looked confused. "What do you mean?"

"I mean you just disappeared on poor Bay here," she challenged him. "That's not a very nice thing to do." I was uncomfortable being referred to as "poor Bay" – but I honestly wanted to hear his answer.

"I didn't disappear," Landon shot back quickly. "I was recovering from a gunshot wound."

"That's your excuse?" Aunt Tillie didn't look impressed.

"It's not good enough for you? I did get shot saving you, after all?" Landon reminded her.

"I didn't need you to save me," Aunt Tillie harrumphed. "I had the situation under control."

As unstoppable as she is, even I had doubts about her ability to stop a bullet with only her mind as a weapon. The doubts were relatively weak, though.

"I'm sure you could have handled the situation," Landon conceded, flashing his dimples again.

"Those don't work on me," she warned him.

"What don't?"

"Those dimples," Aunt Tillie said.

"I'm surprised you can see them with the sunglasses on," Landon countered.

Thistle, Clove and I all sucked in a sharp breath. Landon seemed surprised by our reaction. It didn't stop him from asking the question that we were all mentally warning him against. "Why are you wearing the sunglasses?"

"I'm sick," Aunt Tillie announced.

"That's terrible," Brian interjected with an overt sympathy that could only be described as fake. "Do you have an eye infection?"

"No, I don't have an eye infection," Aunt Tillie said irritably. "I'm allergic to oxygen."

Landon looked surprised. Brian looked doubtful. "I don't think that's really a thing," he said.

Thistle and I exchanged dubious looks. "Uh-oh," she mouthed. I was actually kind of curious how Aunt Tillie would react. I was just glad Landon hadn't said it. Aunt Tillie had once boasted she could shrink a man's, um, unit. I didn't want to risk Landon suffering that fate before I saw what he had to offer. Did I just think that? At least I didn't say it out loud.

"Are you calling me a liar?" Aunt Tillie challenged Brian.

"I don't think he's calling you a liar," Clove interjected helpfully. I couldn't help but be a little irritated that she felt the need to race to Brian's aid. I wanted to see Aunt Tillie unleash her full fury on him.

I saw Thistle jerk spasmodically. If I had to guess, she'd kicked Clove under the table. She was clearly on my side -- as far as Brian was concerned, at least.

"You're not a liar," Brian said hurriedly. "You're very old, though. You might be senile."

My mouth dropped open in surprise. No way was Aunt Tillie going to stand for that.

"What did you just say?" Aunt Tillie was incensed.

"Um ... I said that maybe you're senile," Brian looked suddenly uncomfortable. The fact that he was looking at my aunts and mom for help with the situation was humorous in itself. Despite Aunt Tillie's obvious rage, though, he hadn't tried to placate her. You had to admire his guts – or his rampant stupidity.

"He just called me senile," Aunt Tillie turned to me incredulously. I had insinuated that Aunt Tillie was senile several times in the past month alone. I didn't think now was the time to point that out, though.

"What are you going to do about it?" Hey, focusing Aunt Tillie's rage on someone else – someone I didn't trust – could only help me at this point.

Aunt Tillie was suddenly standing. She was either going to curse him or dump his dinner on him. Both were mildly entertaining possibilities. To my surprise, Aunt Tillie turned on her heel and disappeared into the kitchen. I made a move to get up and follow her, but Twila stopped me.

"I'll go."

The entire table watched as Twila disappeared into the kitchen after Aunt Tillie's rage-filled form. She was like a really tiny Hulk when she got like this. "Is she okay?" I couldn't be sure, but I think the young redhead at the end of the table had asked the question.

"She's fine," Marnie said dismissively. No one who shared in our dubious gene pool actually believed that, but we'd all been trained not to alarm the guests when Aunt Tillie went into one of her 'fits.'

Landon slid a curious look in my direction. "What the hell was that?"

"Aunt Tillie is ... persnickety."

"Good word," Landon encouraged me. He leaned in close so only I could hear him for the next part of his statement. "I don't believe you for a second. You're all worried. That old lady is up to something in the kitchen, isn't she?"

"We're not worried," I lied. "She won't do anything." As long as Twila locked up the Belladonna, that was probably a true statement.

"So," Marnie said nervously, trying to change the subject. "I hear you're working on Myron's murder?"

Landon turned to Marnie. "I am. I have a few questions, if you're up to it?"

"What do you want to know?"

"Did you used to date Mr. Grisham?"

"When I was twenty, we dated for about six months," Marnie admitted.

"What can you tell me about him?"

"He could do a full keg stand for two minutes," Marnie said blankly.

Landon looked surprised. I think his face mirrored mine. "You know what a keg stand is?"

"I wasn't always a mother and aunt," Marnie waved off my surprise. "I went to my fair share of parties."

Landon smiled, despite himself. "What else can you tell me?"

"I don't know," Marnie shrugged. "We were young. He was a nice man. We had a lot of laughs. It wasn't exactly a serious relationship."

"What can you tell me about his family?"

"His mom died when he was a baby," Marnie supplied. "His dad was a deliveryman, back when milk was still dropped off at people's doors. I never really saw him that much."

"And where is his father now?"

"He died right before Marcus joined the Army," Marnie answered.

"Is that why he joined the Army?"

"I can't be sure, we had broken up by then, but I would guess that had something to do with it," Marnie said. "He lost the restaurant, too. He wasn't a very good businessman."

"When was the last time you talked to him?" Landon asked.

"I don't know, a couple days ago? I would run into him around town but never really talk to him."

"Why not?"

"Because he was always drunk," Marnie said honestly. "You can't really hold a deep conversation with someone like that."

She had a point.

Landon seemed satisfied with Marnie's answers. He turned his attention to his lasagna and listened in lazily to the conversation buzzing around us. It was pretty mindless, though.

Thanks to the sudden silence, all I could focus on was the warmth emanating from Landon's body due to our close proximity. It was a calming feeling, which surprised me. Usually he was like a coiled snake ready to strike. His relaxation – especially around the nuttiness of my family – was a whole other facet to him.

Unfortunately, the calm that was washing over me was short-lived. It was interrupted by raised voices from the kitchen. What now?

I got up from the table and followed the sound of the voices. When I entered the kitchen I found Twila and Aunt Tillie wrestling over an herb bottle at the sink. "What's going on?"

"She's going to poison him," Twila huffed.

"Just a little," Aunt Tillie grumbled, relinquishing the bottle to Twila.

"You can't poison him," I pointed out. "Chief Terry would know it was you."

Aunt Tillie shrugged and moved to leave the kitchen and go back into the dining room. I didn't trust her for a second. I grabbed her elbow to slow her. "You've never given up this easily in your life."

"I don't have to poison him to make him pay," Aunt Tillie pointed out.

This was true. "If you're going to curse him, can you do something that makes him want to leave the paper?"

Aunt Tillie squared her shoulders resolutely. "I'll see what I can do."

SIXTEEN

*C*hen everyone was back out in the dining room and seated, the conversation became decidedly stilted.

"So, this murder mystery must be big business for both the store and the inn," Landon said finally. I think the uncomfortable pall that had descended on the table, thanks to the return of the omnipresent Aunt Tillie, had forced him to act as a mediator. It was another interesting new facet of his personality. It was weird seeing him interact with normal people. *Well, people who weren't drug dealers and murderers,* I amended myself.

"We're generally pretty busy," my mom replied. "When we have a town event, we usually book up pretty quickly, but we have seventy-five-percent occupancy just about every week."

Landon looked impressed. "This town manages to sustain its tourism business year round?"

"Pretty much," Marnie said distractedly.

"How is that possible?"

"It's the rebranding," I supplied.

Landon slid a sideways look in my direction. "The rebranding? You mean making it a witch town?"

"It's not a witch town," Thistle interjected. "Just think of it like

Salem, Massachusetts. People love the paranormal, and we're just giving them what they love. It's a niche town, not a witch town."

I furrowed my brow at her sudden explanation. It seemed a little out of place given the circumstances. We were just a family sitting around the dinner table, after all. A normal family, for all Landon and the guests knew. We didn't want to pique Landon's suspicion.

"I think of Salem as a witch town," Landon said. "They have actual history, though. This is just a bunch of people playing witch."

Thistle and I exchanged a wary glance. We needed to change the subject pretty quickly – before Aunt Tillie decided to impart her *knowledge* on the assembled guests.

"So what's it feel like to be shot?"

I cast a flabbergasted look in Thistle's direction. She shrugged helplessly. It was probably the first thing that crossed her mind. We're not great under pressure.

If Landon was surprised by the question, he didn't convey it. "It hurts," he admitted.

"I bet," Twila said. "Is it like a sharp, continuous pain, or does it only hurt at first?"

I don't know why Thistle says she's nothing like her mother. Right now, aside from the shades of their hair, I couldn't see a difference between the two of them.

"I don't know," Landon said truthfully. "I was unconscious for most of it. By the time I was awake, I was on a morphine drip."

"Oh, yeah, I forgot about that," Twila said, biting her lip and fidgeting.

"So, there's no witch history here in Hemlock Cove?" Brian asked. He looked disappointed.

"None that's ever been documented," I lied smoothly.

"Really? Because my grandfather said that it was common knowledge that your family dances naked under the full moon to increase your power base and cast spells."

I'm going to kill William – I don't care that he's already dead.

"That's not witch stuff, that's Aunt Tillie's special wine," Thistle said quickly. "She brews it herself."

Landon smiled lazily in my direction. "You dance naked under the full moon?" I could tell the thought intrigued him.

"I do *not*," I said.

"Thistle, Clove and Bay are embarrassed of their bodies," Marnie said. "They just watch while we do it."

I swear, in Marnie's mind that probably sounded better than it actually came out.

"You watch?" I could tell Landon was fighting to keep from laughing.

Did being forced to watch count? "We don't watch … ."

"So you participate?"

"No."

"So you just watch?"

"No."

Crap! This conversation had taken an obnoxious turn.

"Well, which is it?"

"Anyone ready for pie?" I pushed my chair away from the table. Thankfully, the guests at the far end of the table raised their hands. "I'll go get it."

"I'll help," Clove offered, jumping to her feet.

"Me, too," Thistle added.

"We'll all help," my mom said, ushering Marnie and Twila toward the kitchen.

"I won't," Aunt Tillie said from her spot at the end of the table. "I'll entertain the guests instead."

"I think you should help," I said, glancing down at her as I started to move toward the kitchen. It was hard to read what she was thinking through the sunglasses. I wondered, for a second, if that was the real reason she was wearing them.

"I think I'll stay here and keep Brian and Landon company," she said. "It would be rude for all of us just to abandon them."

That had disaster written all over it. "Don't you want to make sure mom didn't burn the pies?"

"I don't burn pies," my mom looked horrified.

I glared at her openly.

"I don't care how dirty you look at me, you know I don't burn pies," my mom sniffed. "Pick a different lie."

My whole family should be locked up.

"Maybe you undercooked them," I offered angrily. "Aunt Tillie hates it when her apples are hard."

"I don't undercook them either, young lady." One look at my mom, hands on hips, frown on lips, and I knew I would be paying for that comment for the next month – at least.

"Aunt Tillie, come in the kitchen because we want to talk to you away from everyone else," Thistle said irritably.

"About what?"

Aunt Tillie was being purposely obtuse at this point.

"We want to talk about what home we're going to put you in and figure out a visitation schedule," Thistle growled.

Even through the sunglasses, you could feel the ire emanating from Aunt Tillie's chocolate eyes. Thistle was in for a particularly obnoxious payback, I figured. Better her than me – unless Aunt Tillie lumped Clove and me in with her, that is.

"Can you *please* go in the kitchen?" Even I was surprised that I managed to maintain an even tone, especially with both Landon and Brian eying us.

"All you had to say was *please*," Aunt Tillie said, climbing from her chair and marching into the kitchen.

If only that were true.

I was surprised when I felt Landon's hand shoot out and catch my wrist. "Your family should be on a reality show," he said.

Great, I could see it now, the *Hags of Hemlock Cove*. Good grief.

I ignored the comment and followed the rest of my family into the kitchen. I reminded myself that this was just another fun evening with the Winchester witches and their bag of family dysfunction. It couldn't last forever, could it?

When we got into the kitchen, I rounded on Marnie, Twila and my mom irritably. "Thanks for helping."

"I don't burn pies," my mom said. "I'm not going to lie and pretend I do."

"You lie and pretend Aunt Tillie is safe to have around the general population," Thistle pointed out.

We were all thinking it; Thistle was the only one to say it. Of course, Aunt Tillie was really going to make her pay now.

"Someone is full of herself this evening," Aunt Tillie said idly. I noticed she was sitting in the wingback chair in the corner. I hadn't even seen her move. She's like a cat sometimes, I swear. A really evil cat. One of those cats that will eat your face if you die in your sleep and it takes a few days to find the body.

I saw Thistle shudder involuntarily. I'll give her credit, though; she wasn't backing down. "Why can't you just work with us, instead of against us, for a change?"

"Oh please, without me this family would have died of stupidity decades ago," Aunt Tillie said petulantly.

"What does that mean?" Now my mom looked angry with Aunt Tillie. Good. Maybe Aunt Tillie would focus her wrath on her nieces first – leaving her great-nieces alone. Unlikely, I know.

"Whose idea was it to turn this place in a bed and breakfast?" Aunt Tillie asked sagely. "You wanted to make it a bakery. Marnie wanted to make it a bathhouse. And Twila? Anyone remember her grand idea to make it a butterfly house?"

"Those were just dreams when we were teenagers," Marnie protested.

"A butterfly house? How were you going to live in a house with butterflies landing on you?" The other two ideas weren't much better, admittedly, but a butterfly house? Really?

"I was going to train them," Twila jutted her lower lip out.

"Don't they only live like twenty-four hours?" Clove asked. "That would have been a little hard to train a new set of butterflies every twenty-four hours."

"That doesn't mean they can't be trained."

Whatever.

"We need to get a grip here people," I changed the subject. "Both Brian and Landon are now suspicious of us."

"So?" My mom's irritation was now placed on me again. Great. "Everyone in town is suspicious of us. Why would it matter now?"

"Bay is worried that Landon won't like her if he knows she's a witch," Aunt Tillie said wisely.

I rolled my eyes despite the truth in the statement.

"We have bigger fish to fry," I said.

"I don't like fish," Twila said.

"We need to figure out who killed Myron, and we need to do it quick," I said. "If it goes on too long, Landon is bound to find out things about our family." Things nobody ever needed to know.

"I do like shellfish, though," Twila reminded us. We all ignored her.

"Well, you were at the crime scene, did you see his ghost?" My mom asked pragmatically.

"No," I shook my head.

"It just happened," Marnie pointed out. "Maybe he hadn't appeared yet."

"That's a possibility," I agreed. "Or maybe his ghost is someplace else. He didn't exactly have a home base."

"Then we'll have to call his ghost to us," Aunt Tillie said simply.

"How?" Clove asked.

"A séance."

"No, no way, no how, no, no and no. Did I say no?" I was shaking my head so vehemently, I was worried it was going to fly off.

"Why not?" My mom looked surprised. "Tomorrow is the full moon. There's no better time to do it."

Thistle and I exchanged knowing looks.

"That is not why you want to have a séance," Thistle said. "You just want an excuse to run around naked under the moon."

"That's an ugly lie," Twila said, casting a disgusted look at her daughter. "You make us sound like deviants."

"It's not a lie," I charged. "You guys will take any chance you can get to go out there and get drunk and dance and drive us crazy."

"I'm a little sad that you would think so little of me," my mom sniffed.

"Why do we have to do a séance?" I whined.

"If you want to solve the case, you have to talk to Myron," Marnie pointed out. "If you want to talk to Myron, you have to find his ghost. The quickest way to call a ghost is a séance, and if you want to have a séance you need a full coven."

I hate it when she makes sense.

"Fine," I acquiesced. "Just a séance, though. No wine. No music. No unnecessary chanting. And absolutely no nudity."

My mom patted my arm reassuringly. "You need to get over your negative body issues, dear. Once you do, you'll figure out that life will be a whole lot easier. Look at us, none of us are scared of a little harmless nudity."

That's because they didn't have to watch things flopping around from our point of view, I thought. Wisely, I didn't say it out loud.

SEVENTEEN

The next morning, I woke up with a killer headache – and a slightly intangible feeling of foreboding. I couldn't decide if the feeling was tied to Myron's death or my dread of the séance this evening. It was probably a combination of both.

The dessert portion of the previous evening had been just as surreal as the dinner portion, and I couldn't help but feel relieved when Landon had left and Brian had retired to his room for the night.

I wasn't looking forward to work today – especially if Brian was going to hound me about my family's freaky performance of dinner theater the night before. I figured I would just tell him we always did stuff like that to entertain the guests. What? Stranger things have happened. Heck, stranger things happened in my family on a daily basis.

When I got to work, I wasn't surprised to see Brian's car already located in the parking lot. I blew out a frustrated sigh and entered the building anyway. I figured putting it off wasn't really an option. It's always better to just rip off the Band-Aid.

I wasn't surprised to see Brian in the newsroom waiting for me.

"Good morning," I greeted him blandly.

"Good morning."

For a second, I thought he was going to ignore the entire spectacle from the night before. I had a newfound respect for him. It didn't last.

"So, what's wrong with your family?"

There are so many answers to that question, none of which I wanted to expound on with Brian.

"What do you mean?" I feigned ignorance.

"All that weirdness at dinner?"

"Oh, we just do that to entertain the guests," I scoffed.

"Really?" Brian didn't look like he believed me. I didn't blame him.

"We try to keep up appearances that we're witches, just to keep business fresh," I explained.

"Oh," Brian looked nonplussed. "That's a good idea. You guys are really good at it. You must practice a lot."

He had no idea.

"And does that Landon guy usually show up and act like a jealous boyfriend?"

Uh-oh. "No, that's a new development," I said easily. "He's not a jealous boyfriend."

"That's good to know."

I didn't like the gleam in Brian's eyes.

"I haven't seen him in a while," I interjected. "We're just kind of feeling each other out."

Brian's smile faltered. "So, you like him?"

"I don't really know him," I shrugged.

"But you want to know him?"

I hated the quandary I suddenly found myself in. I most definitely wasn't interested in Brian – no matter what his intentions were. It wasn't just because Clove was interested, either. I just didn't trust him. On the flip side, though, I didn't want to talk about my personal life with Landon either. Especially since I wasn't sure I had a personal life with Landon. All we had was mindless flirting – and that whole 'saving my life' thing.

"Like I said," I replied evenly. "We're still feeling each other out."

Brian held his hands up in obvious surrender. "Okay then, I'll let you two figure things out."

I was relieved when Brian closed himself away in William's office again. I had no idea what he was doing in there – my guess was color-coding his paper clips – but I was happy to have him out of my hair.

When I got to my office, I wasn't surprised to find Edith and William waiting for me.

"What's up?"

"Have you heard anything else about Myron?" Edith asked.

"Not yet. I'm going to call Chief Terry in a few minutes to see if they have the autopsy results."

"Why are they working so slowly?" William asked. He seemed agitated.

"It's a small town, William. You know that. Besides, I think it only seems slow to you because you're a ghost and you don't have anything to do but sit around and wait."

William shot me a hard look. "That's the meanest thing you've ever said to me."

"I'm sorry. I didn't realize it would hurt your feelings. I figured you already figured that out yourself."

One look at Edith, and her disappointed countenance, and I realized I was being even more witchy than usual.

"I'm sorry," I offered earnestly this time. "It was just a really long night."

"What? Was your Aunt Tillie sacrificing a goat or something?" Edith asked.

Aunt Tillie was one of the few people still alive in Hemlock Cove who had known Edith during her life. To say they didn't like each other would be an understatement. Edith thought Aunt Tillie was the Devil and Aunt Tillie thought Edith had been out to seduce her late husband. Both scenarios were built on germs of truth, I figured. Since Edith had discovered she could leave the newspaper offices, she had periodically dropped in at The Overlook to haunt Aunt Tillie – who could also see ghosts. That was probably one of the reasons Aunt Tillie's fingers were constantly quirking with curses these days.

"No. It was just a really long dinner."

"I was thinking," Edith said. "Wouldn't Myron be a ghost? He died a violent death, after all."

"That doesn't always mean you become a ghost," I supplied.

"Still, there has to be a way to find him, right?"

"We're going to try and call him to us tonight," I admitted.

"How?" William asked nervously.

"We're going to host a séance," I said.

"Like a bunch of witches holding hands around a crystal ball?" Edith asked. She looked freaked out by the concept.

"No, more like a bunch of witches holding hands in a field."

"And then you're going to dance naked?" William looked excited by the prospect, despite himself.

"Yeah, thanks for telling Brian about that, by the way."

William had the good sense to look sheepish. "I had always heard about it, but I had never actually seen it."

"Who did you hear it from?"

"Everyone in town knows," William shrugged. "Most people think you're out there sacrificing animals."

"You wanted to see it?" The thought made me cringe internally.

"You probably don't realize this, but your mother and your aunts are fine forms of the female body."

"They're in their fifties."

"To a ninety-year-old, that's pretty good," William smiled.

Edith looked scandalized. I didn't blame her.

"Aunt Tillie does it, too," I reminded him.

"Your Aunt Tillie used to be quite the looker, too," William explained. "I always thought that your Uncle Calvin was a lucky man to have married her."

Lucky? Henpecked was more like it, at least from what I had heard. I had never met Uncle Calvin. He had died before I was born.

"Do they really run around naked?" Edith was clearly horrified by the mental picture playing in her mind.

"The four of them do," I admitted. Really, whom was she going to tell? "Clove, Thistle, and I do not." There weren't kegs big enough to convince us that was a good idea.

"Why not?" William looked disappointed.

"It's not our thing."

"Well, at least the three of you are using some common sense," Edith sniffed.

"It's a family tradition," William protested. "They should learn to respect their elders."

I was feeling a little creeped out by lecherous William's fascination with family nudity at this point.

"So, do either of you know why Myron joined the Army so late in life?" As transitions go, it wasn't my best, but I couldn't talk about dancing naked with my family much longer without my head imploding.

"He had a restaurant that he bought with the money he got from his momma's inheritance when he got back from college," William said. "He was a good boy, but he didn't know anything about running a restaurant."

"So, when he lost the restaurant he decided to join the Army?"

"Pretty much."

"And he just did one tour?"

"Yeah," William said. "When he came back he wasn't the same boy."

"Was that because of all that stuff he stole from Iraq?" Edith asked.

If Edith and William breathed, I would have felt like all the air had been sucked out of the room. "What stuff did he steal from Iraq?" This was a new piece of information in the puzzle.

"That was just a rumor," William said hurriedly. "There was nothing true about it."

"Everyone in town said that he stole stuff and buried it in Hemlock Cove," Edith argued. She never was good at picking up on verbal cues, but this was ridiculous. William was obviously incensed that she had told me.

"What kind of artifacts?" I asked the question of Edith, but watched William for his reaction.

"I think it was money," Edith said. "That's what everyone said."

"How do you know that?"

"I'm a ghost," Edith said simply. "People say things in front of me that they wouldn't say in front of anyone else."

"But who said it in front of you?"

Edith must have realized, finally, what she had said because she shot an uncertain look in William's direction. "I don't remember," she lied.

"William, what is Edith talking about?" I turned to him expectantly.

"How should I know?" William looked like he was struggling to refrain from verbally lambasting Edith.

"Well, Edith didn't leave this newspaper for decades," I pointed out. "I didn't know anything about any stolen money from Iraq. That pretty much leaves you?"

William avoided my gaze. "I have no idea what you're talking about."

"You look like you have an idea what I'm talking about," I prodded.

"Well, I don't. You need to stay out of other people's business." With those words, William faded away, but not before I could see the anger that was firmly planted on his transparent face.

I turned to Edith. "Was William involved with something he shouldn't have been? Don't you even think about disappearing, Edith!"

Edith ignored me and followed William's lead.

When I was alone in my office, I couldn't help but think that maybe William's death and Myron's murder had more in common than I initially thought. That meant this case was suddenly a lot bigger. *Crap.*

EIGHTEEN

*A*fter William and Edith's suspicious exits, I was even more confused than before. If Myron had stolen money during Desert Storm, why had he been homeless? Why bury it? And how did William know about it? The biggest question of all, though: Where was the money now?

I tried to push those immediate thoughts out of my mind and called Chief Terry in an effort to focus on the practical instead of the amorphous.

"What's up?" He answered the phone tiredly.

"What did you find out from the autopsy?"

"He was stabbed."

Cop humor is only funny to cops. True story.

"Was he only stabbed once?"

"Yeah," Chief Terry blew out a sigh. "We're trying to see if we can get prints off the knife, but it was covered in blood so the techs aren't overly hopeful."

I considered telling Chief Terry what Edith had let slip, but since I didn't have any way of explaining how that little tidbit had fallen into my lap, I decided to keep it to myself for the time being.

"What about tracking down the knife itself?"

"You can buy it at any Wal-Mart. That's not going to help us."

"So, what do you do next?"

"We investigate," Chief Terry said simply.

Since there was nothing else for us to talk about, I started to say goodbye. I was surprised when Chief Terry interrupted me. "So, I heard Landon went to family dinner last night?" There was a certain tone of mischief in his voice.

"How did you hear that?"

"He told me."

"What did he tell you?" I asked suspiciously.

"He said you were all acting batshit crazy. His words, not mine."

"We were acting normal," I replied. Sadly, it was true.

"He said something weird was going on with Aunt Tillie."

Something weird is always going on with Aunt Tillie. Chief Terry knew that as well as anyone. "She was just in a bad mood," I lied.

"So, she doesn't think she's allergic to oxygen?"

Oh, that. "Yeah. I think she's just looking for attention," I said truthfully.

"You didn't tell her that, did you?"

"No. She's the least of my worries right now. Getting her all wound up could be detrimental to everyone, though. We don't need the distraction."

"Still, it took a lot of guts for Landon to sit through a family dinner with the Winchester women," Chief Terry said pointedly.

"What? Now you like him?"

"No, I don't like him. You just have to admire a man who has dinner with you and doesn't run away from Aunt Tillie screaming."

I pondered Chief Terry's words for hidden meaning, and then a thought occurred to me. "Landon's right there, isn't he?"

"No," Chief Terry said. I could tell he was lying.

"Tell Landon that a brave man doesn't ask another man to do his dirty work." I hung up the phone disgustedly. Men.

I left The Whistler with the intention of going to Hypnotic and telling Thistle and Clove what I had found out. Instead, though, I took a brief detour into Mrs. Little's store. At the age of eighty-three, Mrs.

Little knew a lot about Hemlock Cove – and the denizens of the quiet little hamlet.

Mrs. Little seemed surprised when she looked up from her reading chair by the fire and saw me standing in her small store. "What are you doing here?"

"I have a question," I admitted. Mrs. Little can smell a lie like a fart in a sleeping bag. I figured out, a long time ago, it's better to just play things straight with Mrs. Little.

"What question?"

"How well did you know Myron?"

Mrs. Little looked surprised. "As well as anyone, I guess," she said finally.

"Were you surprised when he joined the Army at such a late age?"

Mrs. Little considered the question seriously. "Yeah, we all were. He didn't have anything left here, though. I guess it made sense for him."

"And when he came back, what did you think?"

"At first, I thought he was just a little lost," Mrs. Little said. "I didn't think much of it. I figured he'd seen a lot during the war."

"And after?"

"He didn't start drinking all at once," Mrs. Little said. "It was a gradual thing. By the time the town realized what was going on, it was too late."

The way she had said the words made me realize Mrs. Little thought I was blaming her – or the town as a whole – for what had happened to Myron. Suddenly, the hundreds of pewter unicorns adorning the shelves seemed to be glaring at me. "I'm not blaming you," I said hurriedly. "I'm just trying to understand how he went from hometown hero to town drunk?"

"If you could understand that, we would all be better off," Mrs. Little said honestly. She had a point.

I wasn't sure how to ask the next question, so I decided to ask around it instead. "Were there any rumors about Myron when he returned from the war?"

"Like what?"

AMANDA M. LEE

"I don't know," I hedged. "About things he'd done over there. Anything he would have brought back?"

"You're asking about the money?" Mrs. Little said knowingly.

"I may have heard someone mention him bringing artifacts back from the war," I admitted.

"I heard it was a big bag of gold," Mrs. Little supplied.

"Gold?"

"That's what everyone said," Mrs. Little replied. "I didn't believe it, though."

"Why not?"

"If he had gold, why would he be homeless?"

I shrugged. "Maybe he felt guilty about stealing it?"

"Maybe," Mrs. Little said, pursing her thin lips. "Still, I don't believe it. He was a drunk. He would have told someone when he was inebriated one night."

That was another very good point. Of course, he could have told William, and that could be what he was hiding. I didn't say that to Mrs. Little, though. Instead, I thanked her for her time and headed toward Hypnotic. I wasn't ready for the chaos I walked in on.

"What are you going to do?" Clove's high-pitched wail could have awakened the dead – which wasn't a good idea when you were in close proximity to me.

"What's wrong?" I asked in alarm, scanning the store for signs of locusts – or Aunt Tillie.

Clove looked relieved when she saw me. "It's horrible," she admitted.

"What's horrible?"

"I don't know how she did it, but she did it."

Clove wasn't making any sense. That happened on a regular basis, but the horror on her face was enough to send a chill through my body.

"Who did what?"

"Aunt Tillie," Clove whispered. I think she thought if she said the name too loud the ceiling would cave in or something. Hey, it wasn't out of the question.

104

"What did she do now?" I looked Clove up and down. She looked the same as usual. A quick shot of fear coursed through me and I glanced at my own reflection in the mirror on the wall. Thankfully, my mustache hadn't grown back. Whatever Aunt Tillie had done – it was only to Thistle. I couldn't help but feel relieved.

"She cursed Thistle," Clove said.

"I'm going to kill her!" Thistle was behind the curtain that led to the storage room in the back of the shop. I hadn't seen her yet – and I wasn't sure I wanted to.

"What did she do now?" I thought about walking behind the curtain, but I figured I would just let the most recent catastrophe come to me for a change. There was no sense in seeking it out.

"What do you think she did?" Thistle challenged from behind the curtain.

I thought about it. Really, with Aunt Tillie, it could be anything. "She didn't give you a wart on the end of your nose, did she?" Aunt Tillie wasn't into repeating curses, but she had pulled the 'wart' gag out a number of times over the years. When she had cursed Clove with one a few years back, she'd enhanced the curse to include three coarse hairs and a curious green hue.

"No. Worse."

"She didn't make hair grow from your ears, did she?"

I saw Clove shudder. That one had plagued her for an entire month.

"No. Worse."

A memory surfaced, one I had tried to bury for eight years. "It doesn't burn when you pee, does it?"

I heard the curtain to the storeroom squeak as Thistle yanked it open angrily. "No. Worse."

"Oh, holy God," I said when I saw her face. "Are those ... are those chicken pox?"

Please be chicken pox. If they weren't, I had no idea what plague Aunt Tillie had set upon Thistle that would make her whole face break out in such a manner.

"I've already had the chicken pox," Thistle gritted out. "We all had them at the same time, remember?"

How could I forget? Our mothers had duct-taped oven gloves on our hands to keep us from scratching our faces. It was a horrific two weeks.

Clove stepped closer to Thistle – but not close enough to touch her, I noticed. I didn't blame her. It could be catchy. "I think it looks like hives," she said finally.

"I don't care what it is," Thistle said. "That old lady better start running now!"

As frightening as Aunt Tillie was, Thistle was more terrifying right now. I don't know who I would pick in a fair fight. My choices were a twenty-three-year-old with age and rage on her side, or an eighty-five-year-old woman with evil on her side. It was going to be a tough call.

Welcome to the Winchester Witches War of 2013. May the Goddess have mercy on all our souls.

NINETEEN

Getting Thistle home without anyone in town seeing her – especially Marcus –proved to be more problematic than initially thought. At first, we had ushered her out the back-door and piled her into the backseat of her car for the drive home. When the car wouldn't start, though, things got more complicated.

"Aunt Tillie strikes again," Thistle seethed.

"How can she break a car?" Clove looked dubious.

"It's Aunt Tillie," I pointed out.

"Good point."

I left Thistle and Clove in the alley behind the store and ran to the newspaper parking lot to get my car. Unfortunately, I ran into Marcus during my mad dash to secure a vehicle that actually worked – hopefully.

"Hey, Bay," he greeted me amiably.

"Marcus," I said nervously.

"Do you know where Thistle is? I tried calling her, but she's not answering her cell phone."

"Um, did you check the store?"

"Of course." Marcus was watching me curiously. He could tell I was freaked out – and out of breath from the sprint to The Whistler.

Thistle had warned me, in no uncertain terms, that I wasn't supposed to dillydally. I don't know if it was the pox on her face, but I was more scared of her than usual.

"It's locked up," Marcus said.

"Did you try the inn?"

"Why would she go to the inn in the middle of the day? No one is sick, are they?"

Define sick. "I don't know where she is," I lied.

Marcus looked momentarily lost. I felt sorry for him – and considered telling him Thistle was fine, for the most part – but the mere thought of Thistle's fury steadied me. This was her business, I reminded myself.

"If I see her, I'll tell her you're looking for her," I said.

Marcus said his goodbyes and walked dejectedly back toward the stables, kicking a few errant rocks as he went. He had it bad for Thistle, I realized. I had no idea how she was going to explain her face to him, though. An allergic reaction? I'd used that excuse several times over the course of my life thanks to Aunt Tillie.

After loading Clove and Thistle in the car – with the latter crouching down in the backseat so no one could see her – I told my cousins what I had found out about Myron.

"No way," Thistle said from the backseat. All I could see in the rearview mirror was a flash of purple hair from time to time.

"What does this mean?" Clove asked nervously.

"I don't know," I admitted. "Hopefully we'll be able to call Myron tonight and get some answers."

"That's after we fix my face, right?" Thistle asked desperately.

"Of course," I said. *Hey, priorities people!*

When we got back to the guesthouse, Clove busied herself grinding up herbs for a poultice while Thistle threw herself on the couch dramatically. "I'm blinded by rage, so I can't tell if I'm overreacting, but I could kill her and get out of jail time because it's justifiable homicide, right?"

"Totally," I agreed.

It took Clove about an hour to finish her poultice. After she spooned it on Thistle's face and admonished her to lie still on the couch for the next two hours – while it did its work – we all sank into an uneasy silence.

Clove was a master at making potions and creams, but we had no idea if her newest concoction would work on a magical malady. In an effort to keep Thistle calm, we eventually acquiesced to her blood-thirsty revenge fantasies.

"We could sneak in and cut her hair while she sleeps," Clove suggested.

"That will just piss her off," I pointed out.

"We could bind her magic," Thistle suggested.

That was an interesting idea. "Are we strong enough to do that?"

"Probably not," Thistle admitted. "She says we're not strong witches because we never use our gifts. Maybe we could get our moms to help?"

"They won't," I interjected. "They're scared of her – and if it doesn't work they'll worry she will come after them. Besides, they're all about that whole respecting your elders crap."

The next two hours crawled by. Finally, Clove instructed Thistle to go and wash the poultice off her face. When she came back out into the living room, we were all relieved that the marks had noticeably faded. They hadn't entirely disappeared, though.

"You can probably cover them up with makeup," Clove said helpfully.

"Until they go away, I guess any sleepovers with Marcus are out of the question," I said.

"Why?" Thistle looked horrified. After seeing him without his shirt, I could understand why.

"He'll see you in the mornings without your makeup," I pointed out.

"That evil, evil old lady."

Clove and I helped Thistle apply her makeup. Thankfully, Thistle was an aficionado of makeup – so she usually wore a decent amount of it. When we were done, you actually couldn't see the marks on her face unless you were really close – and directly looking at them.

"You could apologize," Clove suggested.

"I'd rather die," Thistle swore.

I didn't blame her. Aunt Tillie was getting more and more out of control. Something had to be done.

Instead of going to the inn for dinner – none of us wanted to be around Aunt Tillie – we had a simple meal of tomato soup and grilled cheese at the guesthouse. We spent the next few hours trying to distract ourselves with television and left to go to the clearing shortly before midnight.

The clearing is technically made by nature – and perfected by man, or witch, rather. It had been enhanced over the years, though, with bright gardens and herb beds. There are several rock formations built into the earth, though, that give the area an eerie feeling. That was actually good, because we didn't want random people stumbling across it. Aunt Tillie had actually put a spell on the clearing that would make anyone who was not a witch inexplicably queasy. The spell had worked for thirty years.

What? Aunt Tillie is brilliant and evil all wrapped in a tiny and terrifying package.

We weren't surprised to find that our mothers were already in the clearing preparing for the night's séance by distributing candles in the shape of a circle on the ground. There was no sign of Aunt Tillie.

"Where's the Wicked Witch of the Midwest?" Thistle barked out irritably.

"Who?" My mom asked.

"Aunt Tillie," I supplied.

"She'll be here in a minute. She was watching Jay Leno."

"Did she tell you what she did?" Thistle asked accusingly.

"What did she do?" My mom looked up in alarm.

"She cursed Thistle with some sort of pox on her face," I said.

Twila and Marnie moved to Thistle's side to see if they could see the traces of Aunt Tillie's latest curse. It was hard under the dim light. "Did you make a poultice?" Marnie asked Clove.

"Yeah. It got rid of most of it. You can still see it underneath the makeup, though."

"You did a good job," Marnie said.

"That's all you have to say?" Thistle asked incredulously.

"You can barely notice, dear," my mom patted Thistle's arm dismissively.

So not the point.

Thistle, Clove and I stood back and watched our moms ready the clearing. They were an efficient trio. None of them had to speak to each other; they all just mentally understood what had to be done. After a few minutes, I could hear Aunt Tillie making her way through the woods.

"Let's get this over with," she announced as she stepped into the clearing.

I put an arm on Thistle's hand to stop her from jumping on Aunt Tillie and strangling her on the spot. There would be time for that later.

Aunt Tillie smiled in our direction, although I couldn't see if the smile made it to her eyes since she was still wearing her sunglasses. "How did you make it out here in those?"

"I am at one with nature. I always have been."

"You're at one with evil," Thistle grumbled.

"We're ready," Marnie broke in, trying to defuse the tension.

We all took our spots in the circle. I noticed that my mom and Marnie had wisely put Aunt Tillie between them, and away from Thistle. That was probably the smartest thing they could do at this point, I figured.

Whenever we found ourselves in the circle – especially with the power of the full moon bolstering us – things just happened naturally. Aunt Tillie took on her usual dramatic tone, calling to the earth, wind, water and fire as she wove a web of magic that settled over all of us in a glittery sheet that only we could see.

After a few minutes of chanting, Aunt Tillie started to call for Myron to come to us. I waited expectantly, but nothing happened.

"Now what?"

"Shhh."

I rolled my eyes in Thistle's direction. The theatrics in this family got old pretty quick.

"We're calling to you Myron. We're ordering you to come."

"Ordering?"

"We want to help you cross-over. Come to us. Let us set your soul free."

Good grief.

The lit candles suddenly flickered and then the flames shot up nearly three feet into the air. I drew in a breath as I felt a frostiness encumber the air and descend on the circle. Myron was here – or someone was.

I opened my eyes to see Myron's grizzled face in the circle. He didn't look happy to see us.

"What do you want?"

"We want to talk to you," I said simply.

"Is he there?" Clove asked, obviously confused. I had forgotten she couldn't see ghosts – even if we called them.

"He's here," I said.

Thistle and Clove closed their eyes in concentration. In a few minutes, they should be able to hear him, if history held any bearing, that is.

"What the hell is going on?" Myron asked, looking around at the seven of us. "Are you guys witches or something? I can't hang around witches. People will talk."

"You're dead. Who are they going to talk to?"

"I'm dead?" Myron looked shocked.

When he fainted a few seconds later, I think we were all shocked.

TWENTY

"Vhat happened?" Thistle was looking between Aunt Tillie and me.

"I think he fainted," I answered.

"Can ghosts faint?"

I shrugged. I had no idea.

I watched as Aunt Tillie shuffled over to Myron's prone form and stared down into his face. "He's playing possum," she said finally.

"What?"

"He's pretending," Aunt Tillie said.

"Why would he do that?"

"I can't be seen talking to witches," Myron said from his position on the ground. He still had his eyes screwed shut and was refraining from moving.

"Get up," Aunt Tillie admonished him. "You're embarrassing yourself."

"I'm embarrassing myself?" Myron opened one eye. "You're chanting in a circle in the woods."

He had a point, but no one had taken their clothes off yet, thankfully.

"Get off the ground," Aunt Tillie ordered.

Myron sighed as he got to his feet – actually, it was more like I blinked and he was suddenly on his feet. It was a weird effect.

"Am I really dead?" He asked.

"Could you do that when you were alive?" I asked.

"What did he do?" Clove asked.

"He kind of blinked into a standing position," I explained.

"You're dead," Aunt Tillie told Myron. "We're trying to figure out how you died."

"He was stabbed," Clove interjected again.

"I was stabbed?" Myron looked incredulous.

"What's the last thing you remember?" I asked him.

"I ... I was at the Stirring Cauldron," he said.

"The bar?"

"Yeah. I had a drink, I had a couple of drinks, and then I was going to go check out the bonfire and that's it. I don't remember anything else."

"You were stabbed a few hundred feet from the bonfire," Aunt Tillie supplied. "Right in front of the library."

"Why are you wearing sunglasses in the dark?"

I was surprised at how well Myron was taking his death.

"I'm allergic to oxygen," Aunt Tillie brushed off the question.

"Then how can you breathe?"

Such a good question.

"Only my eyes are allergic," Aunt Tillie said irritably.

"I don't think that's really a thing," Myron said. "Maybe it's just the pollen in the air? It is allergy season."

If Aunt Tillie could curse ghosts, I figured Myron would be in some real trouble. Instead, I decided to move the conversation along. "Myron, do you have any idea why anyone would want to kill you?"

"No, do you?"

"No," I replied. "That's why I'm asking you."

"What about the money?" Marnie asked.

Myron smiled in Marnie's direction. It was too bad she couldn't see him. "Hi, Marnie. You look really nice."

"Thank you, Myron," Marnie said stiffly.

"Are you seeing anyone?"

"Um, no."

"That's good," Myron said happily.

"It's not like ghosts can date," Clove said sharply. I think she was weirded out by Myron hitting on her mom – which she couldn't see and could only hear.

"Who says?"

"I don't know," Clove said honestly. "I think it's just a rule or something."

"Who makes these rules?"

"There are no rules," I interrupted. If Myron wanted to haunt Marnie, that was his business. We had to tackle the task at hand right now.

"Good," Myron said, never taking his eyes off of Marnie. I didn't have the heart to tell him that she couldn't see him. I would let her explain that later – and I was sure there was going to be a later.

"Myron, I don't know any other way to ask this, so I'm just going to ask it," I started. "Did you steal money while you were in Iraq during Desert Storm?"

"Who told you that?" Myron looked stunned.

"Edith told me."

"Who is Edith?"

"She's a ghost at The Whistler."

"Edith Cooper? That lady that died at her desk like fifty years ago? How would she know?"

"I think William told her," I said. That isn't technically a lie.

"He said he would never tell anyone," Myron whined.

"I think she overheard," I explained quickly.

"When she was a ghost?"

"Yes."

"Huh." Myron seemed lost in thought.

"Is it true?" Aunt Tillie asked brusquely.

"I didn't mean to steal, I really didn't," Myron explained. "I found the bag of gold in a house we cleared and no one else was around, and no one lived there anymore, so I didn't see the harm in taking it."

Instead of interrupting him, I just let Myron tell the story in his own time.

"I figured I could reopen the restaurant when I got back," he continued. "But when I got here, I realized that I couldn't get over the guilt of stealing the money. I decided to hide it. I hoped I would get over the guilt and be able to use it. I just never did."

"Is that why you told William about it? The guilt?"

"Yeah," Myron admitted ruefully. "I figured William would know a way for me to get rid of the money, but in a good way."

"Like giving it to charity?" My mom asked.

"Exactly," Myron replied.

"Well, those were good intentions," Marnie said. I couldn't help but notice that Myron was basking under Marnie's praise.

"So, why didn't you do just that?"

"I couldn't find it," Myron said simply.

"What?"

"You lost it?" Thistle looked incredulous.

"I didn't lose it," Myron disagreed. "I just can't remember exactly where I put it."

"You mean you buried it and forgot where you buried it?" Thistle asked.

"No, I didn't bury it. That would have been stupid. I put it in a cave," Myron seemed proud of himself, like putting it in a cave and forgetting where the cave was located was somehow better than burying it and forgetting where.

"Do you remember where the cave was?" My mom asked.

"If I remembered where, I would have taken the money and given it to a charity," Myron said pragmatically. I couldn't help but marvel at how keen he was – that was when he wasn't bombed on whiskey.

"Do you remember the general area?" I asked.

"Down by the Hollow Creek," he said. "That's all I remember."

The Hollow Creek? That wasn't a small area to search. "Did William know where you hid it?"

"Yeah," Myron said. "He tried to help me look for it. We couldn't find it, though. There are like fifty caves down there. I never did get a chance to thank him for trying to help me before he died."

"He's a ghost, too," I offered, hoping it would give him some solace. "Maybe you can tell him now?"

"He's a ghost?" Myron asked, looking around the circle. "Where is he?"

"He's been hanging around the offices at The Whistler," I answered.

I saw Aunt Tillie stiffen across the circle. She had lifted her head up and tilted it to the side, listening keenly. "Someone is coming."

Myron looked scared, which was ridiculous because he was a ghost, and he disappeared within an instant.

I swung around when I heard a twig crack behind us. We all froze in anticipation for a second, and then breathed a collective sigh of relief when Landon stepped in the clearing. Hey, it was better than some random guest or a murderer coming upon us in the dark.

"What are you doing here?" I blurted out.

"I came to see if you were all dancing in the moonlight," he joked. There was an edge to his voice, though, that I couldn't quite identify. "I guess I'm too early. What are you doing?"

I was scrambling to think up a lie when Aunt Tillie did just that for me. "We're communing with nature."

"With candles?"

"And wine," she said, wandering over to the bag Marnie had left at the side of the clearing and pulling out three bottles of her special brew. I knew it! They had planned this all along.

Landon looked impressed when he saw the bottles of wine. "So you come out here once a month to get drunk and dance naked under the stars?"

I felt his gaze wander up and down my body as he said the words. I felt suddenly uncomfortable with his attention. It was like he was mocking me – or doubting me -- and I wasn't sure which possibility made me feel worse.

"Is there something wrong with that?" Aunt Tillie challenged him.

"No," Landon replied easily.

"Do you want to join us?" Twila asked, grabbing one of the bottles from Aunt Tillie and holding it up to him invitingly.

"No," I answered for him.

Landon regarded me for a second. "Why not? Sounds like fun."

I resigned myself to the rest of the night's activities when I saw Landon settle himself on the ground next to my mom and Twila and start drinking straight from the bottle Aunt Tillie had supplied.

"This is strong stuff," he coughed after the first drink. "I can see how you guys get drunk on this stuff so easily."

I still think he thought the naked dancing was just a funny town rumor. He'd learn soon enough, though, that couldn't be further from the truth. Quite frankly, he deserved it for being such a busybody. The horrors he was about to see would stay with him – forever.

TWENTY-ONE

The next morning, I called Brian on his cellphone and told him I was going to be doing some legwork on Myron's death so I wouldn't be going into the office. Thankfully, he didn't answer, so I could get away with just leaving a voicemail. After last night, Brian Kelly was the last person I wanted to talk to. Seriously, how was I going to explain that I got a lead from a ghost?

I showered quickly, dressing in warm layers for the trek I had planned. I was going to visit the Hollow Creek – and see if I could find Myron's cave. I figured if I could find the gold, maybe it would hold a key to who tried to kill Myron. Actually, I just wanted to see if I could find it. What? Who hasn't watched *The Goonies* and then tried to find buried treasure?

When I left my bedroom, I found Thistle and Clove waiting for me in the living room. They, too, were dressed in standard jeans, warm sweaters and heavy hoodies. "What are you guys doing?"

"We're going with you," Thistle said simply.

"What about the store?"

"Our moms are watching over it for the afternoon. They knew we wanted to go with you, so they volunteered."

"They probably just want to redecorate," I said. "They've been hinting at it for a year, and with you two gone for a couple hours, now is their chance."

Thistle's face went ashen. Under the light of day, I could see that the marks from Aunt Tillie's curse had completely faded. She glanced at Clove doubtfully. "They wouldn't, would they?"

"No," Clove said dismissively. I could see the worry lining her face, too. "We can always change it back," she added.

"Why do you really want to go?" I asked them suspiciously.

"Goonies never say die," Thistle snickered.

"What?" I could feel my face begin to redden.

"You love that movie," Thistle said. "I knew that you were going on an adventure to save the Goon Docks – or find the pirate ship – or whatever. How could you possibly resist?"

They knew me too well.

Instead of arguing with them further, I decided to accept their help. The Hollow Creek was a big area. The odds of me just stumbling on a cave in the middle of nowhere by myself weren't great.

As we made our way out to my car, I couldn't help but notice that Clove was lugging a large thermos with her. "What's in there?"

"Hot chocolate," she said.

"Why are you bringing hot chocolate?"

"Why not?"

"It's not exactly like we're going on a picnic," I pointed out.

"It's Rocky Road flavored," Clove teased.

"Really?"

"Yup."

"That's pretty awesome," I admitted.

The Hollow Creek is a remote area located about twenty minutes outside of Hemlock Cove. It's a beautiful panorama, with sandy beaches on the banks of the small river that flows through it. For years, the town had been trying to think of ways to include the area in various town activities. The problem was, it was so remote that there was no way random tourists could find their way to it. Essentially, it had just become a private haven for town denizens who loved the outdoors.

"Marcus said this is the best fishing in the area," Thistle said when we were all grouped on the banks of the river about a half an hour later.

"He fishes?" Actually, that didn't surprise me. Marcus had the look of someone who spent a great deal of time in the outdoors.

"He does. He says he's going to fry fish for all of us one night."

"You don't like fish," I pointed out. "None of us do."

"We can pretend for one night," Thistle protested.

I wrinkled my nose in distaste. I would have to find an excuse to miss fish night.

"Should we split up?" Clove was looking across the small creek uncertainly. It really was a big area.

"I don't know," I said doubtfully. "If we split up, someone could easily get lost ."

Clove didn't look like she liked that idea one bit.

"We could cast a joining spell?" Thistle suggested.

Actually, that wasn't a bad idea. A joining spell didn't actually join us together; it just made us hyperaware of those to whom we were joined. If one of us happened to wander away, the other two would be able to find her.

The three of us clasped hands in a small circle and concentrated. "Three hearts, three minds, one destination," we chanted. "So mote it be."

A slight jolt coursed through all three of us before we separated. "Let's test it, just to make sure," I suggested.

"It's never failed us before," Thistle countered.

We had actually cast the spell numerous times as teenagers. Hey, when you're drunk in a field and there are horny boys all around, you can never be too careful.

The three of us separated, heading in different directions. "Try to stay within shouting distance," I admonished them.

Thistle waved me off dismissively. "Thanks, *Mom*."

While the sandy areas alongside the Hollow Creek are easy to maneuver, the wooded areas on either side are much harder to navigate. Through the years, trees have toppled and the undergrowth has sprouted into dense foliage that is sometimes dangerous to step in. The search of the area surrounding the creek was a lot harder than any of us initially thought it would be.

After about two hours, we hadn't found anything. "I think we should cast a finding spell," Clove suggested.

Thistle and I exchanged wary looks. "I don't know," I hedged. "What happens if someone sees?"

A finding spell is vastly different than a joining spell – which eventually dissipates on its own. A finding spell actually involves conjuring an actual element – usually wind – and giving it a physical form. It *doesn't* dissipate on its own either.

"No one is out here," Clove argued.

"Yeah, but what if it gets away from us – like it did during that Easter egg hunt that year?" Thistle asked.

"We were kids then. I think we're smarter witches now," Clove countered. "Plus, what are the odds that a grown man dressed like an Easter bunny will see it and think aliens have landed?"

That was actually up for debate – the 'smarter witches' thing. I looked at Thistle for a sign of her opinion. She shrugged. "Why not?"

Unlike the joining spell, a finding spell doesn't require a circle. Clove closed her eyes, muttered a few verses, and then snapped her fingers. A small ball of light appeared over her right shoulder. Our element.

"What was with the snap?" Thistle asked.

"It's just something new I'm trying."

"It's pretty lame," Thistle said.

Clove glared at her. "It's not lame." She turned to me. "Is it lame?"

"More cheesy than lame," I interjected.

"That's so much better," Clove muttered. "You always take her side. I know you really think it's cool."

Thistle and I watched Clove expectantly. "What?" She asked irritably.

"You conjured it, you control it," Thistle reminded her.

"Oh, right."

Clove turned to her little ball of light. "There's a cave with a treasure, see if you can find it."

We all stood together and watched as the ball of light zipped away and started exploring various areas around the creek.

"It sounds like it's humming," Thistle said after a few minutes.

"I tried to make it sound like a cicada," Clove admitted.

"Why?"

Clove shrugged. "I just thought it would be cool."

Since the ball of light was now doing all the work, the three of us sat down on a fallen tree and opened Clove's hot chocolate. It was a beautiful day, but you could feel fall starting to take over the weather pattern. The leaves had started turning weeks ago. Soon, the frost would not only start but stick. And then the snow would come. While winter in Northern Lower Michigan is beautiful, it's also my least favorite time of year. I don't do well in the cold.

After about twenty minutes, during which time we saw Clove's ball of light crossing back and forth over the creek in its endless search, we were all startled by the sound of something big moving in the woods behind us. We jumped to our feet and scanned the area, looking for a glimpse of what was coming our way.

"It's probably just a deer," Thistle said nervously.

"Deer don't usually make that much noise," I said.

"Maybe it's a bear," Clove said hopefully.

"Get rid of the finder," I ordered.

"We're not even sure what it is," Clove protested.

"Now," I ordered.

"She's right," Thistle said. "Better safe than sorry."

Clove sighed and snapped her fingers. The low frequency humming dissipated immediately. Okay, the snapping thing was kind of cool.

A few seconds later, a tall figure stumbled from the woods and into the clearing where we were standing. I should have been surprised when I saw who it was. I wasn't, though.

"Landon? What are you doing here?"

Landon looked surprised when he saw us. "Did anyone just see a giant firefly?"

Uh-oh.

"No," I scoffed. "Maybe you're still hung-over from last night?"

Hey, it was a possibility. Those not familiar with Aunt Tillie's special blend usually ended up on their asses – or on their knees over a toilet. Landon had imbibed half a bottle of wine himself last night. That probably saved him when the naked dancing began. I could only hope he had blocked it out – whether the alcohol had done it or his mind had done it as a defense mechanism.

"I'm not hung-over," Landon argued, although I noticed he looked paler than usual and the circles under his eyes were pronounced. "Speaking of that, though, what happened last night?"

"You got drunk and we put you to bed on the couch in the back-room of the inn," I said.

"I didn't drink that much," Landon protested.

"Aunt Tillie's special blend isn't meant for mere mortals," Thistle said.

"You guys seem fine," he countered.

"We're used to it – and three drinks is our limit. That's three sips. We know better than guzzling it."

Landon rubbed his head ruefully. "I guess so. It's not like you guys didn't warn me."

"What are you doing out here?" I repeated the question. I was suddenly suspicious of Landon's unplanned arrival.

"Your Aunt Tillie said you were down here looking for clues," Landon said. "Although, I can't figure out why. She sent me down here."

"And you listened?"

"She doesn't seem like she understands the word no."

Good point.

"So, what are you looking for?"

Thistle and Clove were suddenly fascinated with their boots. *Great. What the hell am I going to tell him? Oh, screw it.* "There's an old town rumor that Myron stole gold from Iraq when he was in Desert

Storm. He spent a lot of time down here over the years, so we thought it was worth a look."

What? The explanation made us sound stupid, not like witches.

Landon narrowed his eyes. "Why haven't I heard about this before?"

"I just told you," I countered.

Landon sighed, shaking his head irritably. "Have you found anything?"

"No."

I glanced over to Thistle, but she was staring up at the sky darkly. "It's about to storm," she said.

"How can you possibly know that?" Landon asked as he glanced skyward.

We didn't answer. It wasn't necessary. The rumble of thunder that followed did it for us.

"It's going to be a bad one," Clove said nervously.

"We won't be able to make it back to the car," I said. "We have to find shelter."

Landon looked at us all like we had each sprouted a second head. "Has anyone ever told you that you're weird?"

Just everyone we'd ever met.

Thistle and I quickly started feeling our way along the thick trees. Hopefully we would be able to find somewhere in the underbrush to take shelter. "Hey," Thistle said suddenly. "I found a cave."

Great. If only we would have found it before Landon arrived. Landon made his way to our side, helping us clear the tree branches from the narrow opening. "You want me to go in there?" I couldn't help but notice the quiver of fear that shook his voice.

"Are you scared of the dark?" Thistle asked.

"No," he scoffed. "I just don't like enclosed spaces."

"You're claustrophobic?"

"No," Landon said, squaring his shoulders as the skies opened up and a downpour began. "I'm fine."

We all stepped into the cave. The opening was so narrow we had to go single file. I grimaced when I realized I was at the front of the line. When we all were under the protective cover of the rock, I turned to Thistle. "Do you have a lighter?"

"Yeah," I heard her digging through her pockets.

I used the lighter to continue into the cave, silently using my power to sustain the small flicker so it wouldn't blow out. I could only hope Landon wouldn't notice.

"Why are we going into the cave?" Landon asked.

"We might as well look around," I pointed out. "There's nothing else to do."

Thankfully, the narrow passageway widened a few feet in. After walking a few more feet, we stepped into a much wider cavern. Unfortunately, the small light from Thistle's lighter wasn't letting us get a very good glimpse of our surroundings. "We should have thought to bring a lantern," I said finally.

"Next time," Thistle agreed.

I could sense her moving to my left. The joining spell was still working. "Ow!"

"What is it?" Clove asked in a panic.

"I ran into the wall."

"Don't do that. You'll give me a heart attack," Clove grumbled.

"Why are you touching the wall?" Landon asked. "There could be snakes or something."

"Are you scared of snakes, too?" I couldn't quite be sure where he was in the darkness, but I shifted in the direction I thought his voice was emanating from. To my surprise, I felt something brush my ass. "Really? You're going to grab my ass now?"

"That's not me," Landon said. He was right; his voice was too far away.

"Very funny, Thistle," I chided her. "I'm going to kick your ass."

"It's not me," she said. Her voice was a few feet away, too.

"Clove?" I asked hopefully.

"Uh-uh," she said. "I'm over by Landon."

"Then ... whose hand is on my ass?" My voice had risen almost three octaves.

"Maybe you just ran into something?" Landon suggested.

That was possible, but I didn't think so. My hands were shaking as I turned slowly and flicked the lighter on. I almost passed out when the empty sockets of a human skull were suddenly illuminated in the small light.

"Holy shit," I breathed. "We found One-Eyed Willie."

I didn't get a chance to hear their responses, because suddenly all the blood was rushing to my brain and darkness was overtaking me as a sustained clanging noise started echoing in my mind. The last thing I remembered was Thistle and Clove rushing forward to catch me so I wouldn't hit the floor of the cave.

The joining spell had enabled them to overcome the dark and find me. I let my own personal darkness overtake me. I just needed a nap, I reassured myself. It would all be fine when I woke up. Being felt up by a skeleton was just going to be a hazy memory.

TWENTY-TWO

*I*t was just a dream, I realized as consciousness started washing over me again. How could it be anything but? If it had been real, I would have been waking up on the cold floor of the cave. Instead, I was waking up on a soft surface and I had a warm blanket placed over me. It had all been a dream. Just a really bad dream.

"Get up! You've slept half the day away! This is not how Winchester women approach life."

Welcome to my nightmare. What the hell was Aunt Tillie doing in my bedroom? I opened my eyes slowly, the sudden light causing brief blurriness. When Aunt Tillie's angry face swam into view, I suddenly wished for a case of hysterical blindness. "What happened?" I croaked.

"You fainted, again, and made an ass out of yourself," Aunt Tillie replied. "Again."

"I wasn't asking you," I grumbled.

"You fainted when you saw the skull," Clove said sympathetically. "Landon carried you out of the cave, through the storm and then drove you here. He wanted to take you to the hospital, but we told him Aunt Tillie would be able to take care of you."

"Why would you tell him that? She's not exactly known for her bedside manner."

Clove ignored the question.

"Where is Landon now?"

"He went back to the cave with Chief Terry and a crime scene team," Thistle said.

"So, it really was a skull?"

"Yeah," Thistle said. "It really was a skull. You didn't imagine that."

"Next time I fancy myself a Goonie, remind me of this," I said, struggling to sit up. I looked around the room and realized I was in the living quarters of the inn.

"What's a Goonie?" Aunt Tillie asked.

"Never mind," I grumbled.

"Is that some sex thing you think goes right over my head because I'm old?" She asked obnoxiously. "I'm on to you."

"You caught us," Thistle said sarcastically. "Goonie is a code word for sex. You're smarter than all of us combined."

"No one needs your tone," Aunt Tillie admonished Thistle.

After Aunt Tillie force fed me two bowls of her homemade chicken noodle soup, she finally agreed to let the three of us leave – but only if we promised we were only going back to the guesthouse and not going to get into another round of trouble. "It's time for my nap," she sniffed.

"Where is my mom?" I asked in surprise. I was relieved not to have her hovering, but I couldn't understand why she wasn't here vetoing my outfit choice of the day.

"I sent her down to Hypnotic with Marnie and Twila," Aunt Tillie explained. "She was bugging me."

"She let you run the inn by yourself?"

"It was only for a couple of hours and all the guests were out at the hayride," Aunt Tillie answered.

Well, that explained it.

"Besides, Thistle and Marnie were trying to move that big display case in the store and they needed help," she said.

Thistle visibly blanched. "I'm going to kill them."

129

"Let it go," Clove sighed. "We'll move it back this weekend. Bay shouldn't be lifting heavy objects right now, anyway."

"How did I get roped into moving furniture with you guys?" I protested.

"It was your idea to go investigating Hollow Creek," Clove pointed out.

"I didn't make you come!"

"What would have happened if we hadn't been there?"

Whatever.

Once we got back to the guesthouse, Clove situated me on the couch. She was acting like a mother hen – and it was annoying. "I didn't hit my head," I pointed out. "You guys caught me."

"You should still rest," Clove said. "This fainting thing is starting to become a regular occurrence with you."

"You just need an outlet for all your nervous energy," I said. "And I've only fainted twice in my life – and both times were under extremely stressful circumstances." Like being shot at by a murderer and being groped by a dead body.

Despite the surreal adventures of the afternoon, the three of us settled in to watch a marathon of *The Walking Dead*. Sure, it was macabre, but it was also a reminder that things could always get worse.

After several hours that consisted of a prison riot, a bloody C-section, and eyeball impalement, we were all jolted to reality by a rapid knock on our front door.

"If that's my mom, tell her I'm already in bed," I ordered Clove as she answered the door.

"It's not your mom," she said, opening the door to let Landon in. He looked exhausted.

"How are you feeling?" he asked.

"Fine."

Landon glanced at the television. "You're watching *The Walking Dead* after the afternoon you had?"

"It's a great show," I shrugged.

Landon shook his head tiredly. "You guys are unbelievable."

"What did you find?"

Landon slid onto the sofa next to me. I couldn't help but notice that he situated himself so our thighs were touching. "Not much. We have no idea who the body belongs to, or how long it has been there. We'll know more tomorrow."

"How did he die?"

"We're not sure it's a he. Whoever it was, though, was stabbed," Landon said wearily.

I raised my eyebrows. "With the same knife that killed Myron?"

"That's a possibility," Landon admitted. "It will take a while to prove, though. Forensics isn't like it is on television. It takes a long time."

"You mean *Bones* isn't real? Any other illusions you want to shatter for me?" I teased.

"You make me tired," Landon grumbled. He looked around the guesthouse curiously. "And hungry. Do you guys have anything to eat?"

"We're feeding you now?"

"We could order pizza," Clove offered.

"That sounds good," Landon said. "I like anything – except anchovies."

"No one likes anchovies," I muttered.

"I'll call Marcus and have him pick it up," Thistle said.

"Marcus?" I raised my eyebrow suggestively.

"He was going to come over anyway," Thistle avoided meeting my gaze. "I'll have him pick up a case of beer, too."

Landon groaned. "None for me. I'm still recovering from Aunt Tillie's brew. Does she have a license to make that stuff, by the way?"

"Why don't you ask her?"

"That's all right," Landon said. "I like my balls where they are."

Marcus arrived at the guesthouse about an hour later. After introducing him to Landon, we all dug into the pizza enthusiastically. The conversation was stilted at first – mostly because we were all stuffing our faces – but when the chewing slowed down the conversation picked up.

"I can't believe you guys found a body," Marcus said. "What were you doing out there anyway?"

I saw Landon lean forward slightly in anticipation of our answer. "We heard a rumor that Myron had hidden money he stole from Iraq out there. We were trying to find it."

"You mean the rumor that he stole money from Desert Storm?" Marcus asked innocently.

"You heard it, too?" Thistle looked surprised.

"It's a small town," he shrugged. "I never believed it."

"We watched *The Goonies* last night and it seemed like a good idea," Thistle lied. "Bay loves *The Goonies*."

"That's a great movie," Marcus agreed. "You should have asked me to go with you. We could have made a day out of it."

"We didn't plan on spending so much time out there," Thistle explained. "The day just kind of got away from us." In more ways than one.

"Yeah, I wondered where you were when I went into the store and found your moms redecorating."

Thistle swallowed hard. "Exactly how much redecorating did they do?"

Marcus looked confused. "I don't know. It was hard to tell with everything spread all over the store like it was."

Thistle pinched the bridge of her nose to stave off a headache. "I'm going to kill them."

"I thought they were just being nice," Marcus said, cracking open a beer. "I'm sure they were just trying to help."

He was handsome, but naïve. If he spent much more time around our family, he would learn.

"They seem a little crazy to me," Landon said, reaching for his own beer.

"I thought you weren't going to drink," I reminded him.

"Your family drives me to it," he said, taking a long pull from his bottle. "Dancing naked under the moon is just the tip of the iceberg."

"You remember that?"

"Who could forget? It was nightmare inducing."

"You saw them dancing naked?" Marcus looked surprisingly jealous.

"Just the moms and Aunt Tillie," Landon grimaced.

Marcus looked horrified. "Really?"

"Yeah."

"How was it?"

That was an odd question.

"Exactly how you would expect it to be," Landon said, slamming the rest of his beer. "There are things you should never see in life – and that was one of them. Aunt Tillie especially," he shuddered. "Just imagine things spinning in opposite directions that should never be spinning at all."

I couldn't help but laugh at the twin horror expressions on their faces. Welcome to our world.

TWENTY-THREE

"*W*hat is this? A whorehouse?"

I bolted awake at the sound of my mom's voice. It took me a second to realize where I was, and then everything hit me – including the pain shooting through my back from sleeping on the floor.

I glanced around the room, trying to get a grip on exactly what was going on. I saw Thistle and Marcus asleep on the floor a few feet away – complete with Marcus' hand cupping Thistle's breast. *Nice.* Clove was stirring on the couch behind me, which meant the body on the floor beside me – the really warm body with an arm draped over my hip must be ....

"Good morning," Landon mumbled sleepily, his dark hair dipping over his partially opened eyes. "What was that shrieking? Do you guys have a cat? Or one of those really annoying yipping dogs that I don't know about?"

"My mom." *Crap.* My mom.

I glanced up to the open front door of the guesthouse and frowned when I realized she wasn't alone. Twila and Marnie were with her, and they were all standing, hands on hips, with curious looks on their faces. Actually, the looks were more murderous than curious.

"Don't you knock?"

"This is our property," my mom reminded me. "Which we let you live on rent free, in case you forgot."

Like they'd ever let us.

"What time is it?" Thistle asked, gazing up at the three scowling faces in the doorway. She must have realized where Marcus' hand was, because she hastily brushed it away.

"It's almost noon," Twila barked. She was glowering in Marcus' direction.

I glanced up at the ornate clock on the wall disbelievingly. "It's 9 a.m."

"Close enough," Marnie said.

"Compared to what?" Clove grumbled.

"Does someone want to explain what's going on here?" My mom asked, tapping her foot irritably on the hardwood floor.

"Slumber party?" I suggested. I noticed that Landon had not removed his hand from my hip. The warmth was reassuring in a weird way – especially since my mom and aunts were watching me like I'd just given him a lap dance.

"We had pizza and beer and then passed out," Clove explained hurriedly. She always was the one who worried the most about what our mothers thought.

"Oh," my mom looked relieved. "I thought it was something else."

"Like what?" Thistle asked, struggling to a sitting position. I couldn't help but notice that Marcus was trying to make himself small on the floor in an effort to deflect the disdain that he was certain was coming his way. It was a fruitless endeavor.

"It could have been an orgy," Twila suggested.

"Good grief," Thistle muttered, climbing to her feet. "We're all dressed."

"That could have just been for our benefit," Twila pointed out.

"Since we didn't know you'd be coming here, that seems pretty doubtful," Thistle shot back.

"Don't take that tone with me," Twila warned.

"Oh, leave them alone," my mom admonished her sisters. "Don't you remember what it was like to be their age?"

"Winnie, we never had guys spend the night at the house," Marnie countered. "When we did stuff like this, we had the common sense to do it in a field like everyone else."

"Only because Aunt Tillie wouldn't let us," my mom replied. "If she would have let us, we would have done this and worst."

"True," Marnie said. "Okay, then. Everyone wash their faces and then we'll see you up at the inn for breakfast."

"I have to go to work," I argued.

"Breakfast first," my mom ordered.

I heard Landon's stomach rumble beside me. "What are you cooking?" I asked finally.

"French toast."

"We'll be up there in ten minutes," I said resignedly.

It was closer to fifteen minutes when we finally entered the living quarters at the back of the inn. Neither Marcus nor Landon had ever been in this part of the establishment, so they were understandably curious.

"It's not what I expected," Marcus said finally, looking around interestedly.

"What did you expect?"

"The heads of all their past loves mounted on the walls," Landon muttered.

"I wouldn't be funny like that with Aunt Tillie," I warned. "She doesn't take sarcasm well."

"Does she take anything well?" Landon asked.

Not really. "She's just set in her ways," I said.

"I have a feeling she was like this when she was twelve."

I had a feeling he was probably right.

We led Marcus and Landon through the kitchen – which was already empty – and into the dining room. Everyone was already seated at the table, and no one but Brian looked up when we entered. A smile touched his lips; that is until he saw Landon walk into the room after me. "Late night?" He asked suspiciously.

"You could say that," Landon said slyly, sliding into a chair next to me. "Most of it is just a blur. What I do remember was pretty fun, though."

I shot Landon a bewildered look. I don't know what it is about Brian, but he makes Landon's testosterone shoot through the roof.

"You all spent the night together?" Brian asked uneasily, casting a glance around at the five of us.

"It wasn't what you think," my mom said hurriedly.

"What do I think?" Brian asked.

"It wasn't an orgy," Twila explained. "They all just drank too much and passed out. They had their clothes on. We saw. They have witnesses."

I shook my head disgustedly. "He doesn't need to know that."

"I just want to make sure that people don't jump to the wrong conclusions," Twila said. From the woman who dances naked with her sisters once a month, that was pretty rich.

I glanced over at Landon, who was inhaling his French toast like he hadn't eaten in months. "You want to help out here?"

"What? It could have been an orgy," he said, shooting a dark look in Brian's direction.

"You said it wasn't an orgy," Twila looked horrified.

"Stop saying orgy," Thistle exploded.

"They're too prudish to have an orgy," Aunt Tillie said sagely. "They won't get naked in front of each other, let alone a bunch of guys. They think their thighs are too big."

She had a point.

Aunt Tillie turned to Brian. "It's none of your business if they did have an orgy, anyway. Why don't you try minding your own business? If they want to have an orgy, that's their business."

Landon smiled at me. "I'm really starting to like your Aunt Tillie."

TWENTY-FOUR

$\mathcal{A}$fter breakfast, Landon corralled me outside of the inn by boxing me against the outer wall of the back residence. "Where are you going?"

"What do you mean?" I asked with faux innocence.

"Don't, don't do that," he waved his finger in my face. "It's not cute."

"You don't think I'm cute?"

Landon's eyes turned dark and predatory. "Do you want me to think you're cute?"

Crap. This had taken an unexpected turn. "I haven't decided yet," I said honestly. "Sometimes I do and sometimes I don't really know."

Landon looked me up and down with a knowing look, but he took a step back anyway. "You've decided. You're just not sure you've made the right decision. We'll deal with your crap later. For now, we have a murder to solve."

"We?" I raised an eyebrow. "Suddenly you're involving me in the investigation? What happened to me having no business in an active investigation?"

"I can't keep you out of it," Landon replied. "I've realized that pretty quickly. I figure it's better to keep you close to me than worry about you wandering around sticking your nose where it doesn't belong with no backup."

I opened my mouth to argue, but Landon cut me off. "And Clove and Thistle don't count as backup."

I sighed in defeat. "Fine. What did you have in mind?"

"We're going to see Chief Terry first," Landon said. "Then we'll decide where to go from there."

We hiked up to the guesthouse. I ran inside long enough to grab a coat and a purse and then met Landon back outside. "We're driving together?"

"I'm not letting you out of my sight," Landon shot back. "You'll just end up in trouble if I'm not watching you."

Well, that was insulting. True, but insulting.

When we got to the police station, Chief Terry seemed surprised to see us arriving together. "What's going on?"

"What do you mean?" I asked.

"Why are you two together this early in the morning?" He was obviously suspicious. The dark glares he was shooting in Landon's direction were evidence of that.

"We had breakfast at the inn and decided to drive here together," I said evasively.

Landon shook his head. "I spent the night at the guesthouse."

Chief Terry puffed out his chest like a snarling cat. "You spent the night?"

"We had too much to drink and passed out on the floor," I explained. I had no idea why I felt the need to justify my actions. I just didn't like the disapproving look on Chief Terry's face – even though it was directed at Landon.

"So, you got her drunk and took advantage of her?" Chief Terry turned his ire on Landon.

"How do you know she didn't take advantage of me?" Landon said with faux innocence.

"I've known her since she was a child. She's a pain in the ass, but she's genuinely a good person. I trust her a lot more than I trust you."

I shot a triumphant glance in Landon's direction. Landon rolled his eyes. "We weren't alone. Her cousins were there ... and some guy from the stables."

"Marcus Wellington?" Chief Terry asked.

"He's dating Thistle," I supplied.

"He's a good boy," Chief Terry said approvingly. "They might be a good match. He's patient and she's all over the place. Do your mom and aunts like him?"

"What does that matter?" Landon asked in surprise.

"They're good judges of character," Chief Terry said.

"You're just saying that because they fight over you," I pointed out.

"That shows good taste," Chief Terry shot back.

"They fight over you?" Landon looked doubtful and amused at the same time.

"What do they think about you?" Chief Terry asked pointedly.

"I think they like me," Landon said.

Chief Terry turned to me for confirmation. I shrugged. "They seem to like him – although they weren't thrilled to find him passed out on the floor with us this morning."

Chief Terry chuckled. "They found you?"

"Twila was worried we were having an orgy."

"She's cute," Chief Terry smiled.

Whatever. I decided to change the subject. "What did you find out about the body in the cave?"

Chief Terry wasn't ready to be dissuaded from the previous topic of conversation, though. "So they found you all sleeping on the floor together and yet they still invited you to breakfast?"

"Yes," Landon replied.

"Then they must like you," Chief Terry said. "Maybe you're not as bad as I originally thought."

"What? Just because my mom and aunts like him, now you like him? Way to think for yourself."

Landon glared in my direction. "You're unbelievable."

"So, what did you find out about the body in the cave?" I asked again.

Chief Terry sighed. "Not much. The coroner said that the body has been out there for a really long time. Years. It's going to take a while to identify the body – and get a time of death. All we know right now is that it was a woman."

A woman? Well that was something. "What about a cause of death?"

"That was pretty easy, given the big knife wound in the clothes. The blade actually nicked the sternum."

"So, just one stab wound? Just like Myron?"

"That's what it looks like."

"Was it the same knife?"

"It could have been," Chief Terry said. "The problem is, there is really no way to be sure. The sternum didn't have any flesh on it, so there's no way of knowing if the blades match. All we can be sure of is that the blades were roughly the same size – and the wounds look to have been inflicted in the same manner."

"You believe that the two cases are connected?"

Chief Terry shrugged. "I think it would be one heck of a coincidence for you to stumble upon one body during the investigation of another and not have the two cases be connected. Especially in a town the size of Hemlock Cove."

"Did you find anything else in the cave?" I asked.

"Like a big bag of coins?" Chief Terry searched my face for an answer.

I shot a dark look in Landon's direction. "You told him?"

"Of course I told him," Landon scoffed. "This is an investigation, not a playground game."

I resisted the urge to shoot him the finger and turned to Chief Terry. "What do you think?"

"I don't know," Chief Terry said. "I never believed the stolen money story, for obvious reasons. I can't figure out why anyone would want to kill Myron otherwise."

I bit my lower lip. Chief Terry could tell I was thinking. "What do you know?" He asked suspiciously.

I sighed. "I think William Kelly's death should be looked into," I said finally.

"Why?" Chief Terry seemed surprised.

"Who is William Kelly?" Landon asked in confusion.

"The owner of the newspaper," Chief Terry answered for me.

"That tool Brian's grandfather?"

"Yes."

"Why do you think his death is suspicious?" Chief Terry asked.

How the heck am I supposed to explain this? "I just remembered that Myron spent the night at William's a lot of the time."

"He spent the night at my house, too," Chief Terry pointed out. "He spent the night at everyone's house, for that matter."

I pursed my lips. There really was no rational reason for me to suspect William's death was anything but an accident. I couldn't exactly admit that my interactions with a ghost had led me to believe that something bigger was going on.

Chief Terry must have realized that I was waging an inner battle with my own mind, because he sighed. "I'll have William's body exhumed."

"Just because she thinks the deaths might be linked? Wasn't William Kelly ninety years old?" Landon looked dumbfounded.

"It's a small town," Chief Terry said smoothly. "William died in close proximity, time-wise at least, with Myron. It can't hurt to make sure he died of natural causes. Better safe than sorry, right?"

"Something is going on here," Landon sputtered. "What is the big secret? You guys are hiding something from me."

I ignored him. "My theory is that Myron told at least one person about the money over the years."

"And you think William might be one of them?" Chief Terry surmised.

"He looked at William like a father," I pointed out.

"If that's true, than either William or Myron had to tell at least two other people."

"How do you figure?"

"We have another body in a cave," Chief Terry pointed out. "And if William was murdered, then we have three dead bodies. That still leaves another person out there as a killer."

He had a point.

"Who could it be?" I asked helplessly.

"I figure it has to be someone who knew Myron relatively well, either in the past or the present," Chief Terry said.

"Was he especially close to anyone in town?"

"Not now," Chief Terry said briefly. "However, he didn't go off to the war alone."

"He didn't?" I was surprised. This was the first I had heard about it.

"No. There were several of our young men who joined the Army together that year," Chief Terry said. "Myron was older than the others, but they all went off together as a unit. The other three were the same age as each other, though. They all went to high school together."

"Who?"

"Billy Kelly, Jr. for one," Chief Terry supplied.

"William's son?"

"Yes. He was one of the four. There was also Ken Trask and Mike Wellington."

I felt my heart drop to my stomach. "Mike Wellington? Marcus' father?"

"Yes," Chief Terry nodded.

"Why didn't you tell me this before?"

"I didn't think it mattered," Chief Terry said matter-of-factly.

"What if Mike Wellington, Bill Kelly, Ken Trask and Myron were all in on it together? Stealing the coins, I mean."

Chief Terry shrugged. "That doesn't mean they're all killers."

"Bill Kelly died ten years ago. Mike Wellington died about a year ago. That leaves Ken Trask as the only living member of the quartet," I said. "But what if Bill Kelly told Brian or Mike Wellington told Marcus?"

Chief Terry considered it for a minute. "Brian Kelly did come to town right before Myron was killed."

"And he's been searching William's office for something," I said.

"What do you mean?" Landon asked in surprise.

143

"He says he's been redecorating, but he spends hours in there moving the furniture and tearing things apart," I answered.

Landon exchanged an unreadable look with Chief Terry. "Maybe we should have a talk with Brian Kelly?"

Chief Terry nodded. "It couldn't hurt."

The two of them got to their feet and glanced down at me. "Are you coming?" Landon asked.

"No, I trust you two."

Landon watched me suspiciously. "What are you going to do?"

"I'm going to Hypnotic to find a way to keep Thistle away from Marcus until we're absolutely sure it's not him," I said honestly.

"That's probably a good idea," Chief Terry admitted.

"You're just going to Hypnotic? Nowhere else?" Landon questioned me seriously.

"I'll stay at Hypnotic with Thistle and Clove until I hear from you," I promised.

That was my intention, it really was. Nothing ever goes according to plan in Hemlock Cove, though.

TWENTY-FIVE

*W*hen I got to Hypnotic, Clove was working in the front of the store alone. I figured that Thistle was in the back doing inventory – or bagging herbs – and I wanted to approach Clove first about the Marcus situation. I didn't want to make Thistle unjustly suspicious if I didn't have to. She tends to panic – even when there's nothing to panic about. If there is a legitimate reason to worry, then she's going to fly off the handle like nobody's business.

"So what happened after we left?" I asked Clove.

"Brian Kelly pitched a fit," Clove clucked angrily.

Uh-oh. "What do you mean?"

"He started casting aspersions on Landon's character," Clove said. "Saying that he shouldn't be trusted alone with you. That he's probably some sort of sexual deviant. I think he was jealous."

Well, this wouldn't end well, especially given Clove's crush on Brian. "I don't know why he would be jealous."

"He likes you," Clove said irritably. "He's interested in you. That's obvious, so don't pretend it's not."

"I haven't encouraged him at all," I said hurriedly.

"I know," Clove said sharply.

"He could be the bad guy anyway," I admitted.

"What?" Clove looked shocked.

I told her about what Chief Terry had just told me. She sank down onto the couch heavily when I was done. "Do you think it's him?"

"I don't know," I admitted. "I think his arrival in town is suspicious. He's kind of a goof, though. It's hard to imagine him creeping around killing people and searching through caves for money. He's not exactly an outdoorsy guy."

"Do you think he would really kill his grandfather, though? That's his blood."

"I don't know," I shrugged. "We've all had dreams about killing Aunt Tillie."

"Yeah, but we wouldn't really do it," Clove pointed out. "You wouldn't, would you?"

"No," I said honestly. "Thistle might, though."

"Totally."

"Where is she, by the way? Is she doing inventory in the back?"

"No, she took the day off," Clove said innocently.

"What do you mean?" I couldn't help the pang of alarm that coursed through me.

"She said she had things to do," Clove said. "I didn't ask her what those things were. I figured it was Marcus."

Shit!

"Are they up at the guesthouse?" I got to my feet hurriedly.

Clove looked confused by my sudden action. "I don't know."

I reached into my pocket for my cellphone and swore when I realized I had left the phone in the charger at home. "Call her."

"What?" In our current situation, Clove was obviously three steps behind me in the race to enlightenment and I was running out of patience in the explanation game.

"Call her!"

Clove hurriedly scurried up to the phone and punched in the number to the guesthouse. I watched her nervously. "The voicemail picked up," Clove said. "Should I leave a message?"

"Tell her to call you. Don't say anything else," I warned.

When Clove was done, I took the phone from her and called up to the inn. My mom answered. "Is Thistle up there?"

"Hello to you, too," my mom admonished me.

"Hello. Is Thistle up there?"

"I don't know who taught you phone etiquette, but you clearly didn't learn it from me."

If I could strangle her through the phone, I would. "Is Thistle up there?"

"No. She packed a picnic basket a few hours ago and then left with Marcus. She didn't say where she was going. Why?"

"I don't know," I bit my lip. "I just don't think she should be alone with Marcus right now."

"Why? He seems like a nice boy."

I made the decision in an instant. I gave her an abbreviated version of the story Chief Terry had told me and then waited for her reaction. "You think Thistle is having lunch with a murderer?"

"No," I said hurriedly. "I just want to make sure that she's safe."

"I don't think Marcus could be a murderer," my mom said, although I could hear the doubt creep into her voice. "He's too good looking to be a murderer." It sounded like she was trying to convince herself more than anything else.

"Are you sure she didn't say where she was going?"

"No," my mom said. "What are you going to do?"

"Find her."

I started pacing the store. Where would she go? I turned to Clove suddenly. "The overlook."

"The inn? You just called there and she's not there," Clove's voice was bordering on shrill.

"Not the inn, the actual overlook. Thistle loves it there."

The overlook was a cliff bluff at the far end of our family property. Technically, it's what the aunts had named the inn after and not *The Shining*. As a teenager, Thistle had spent hours up there reading and looking out over Hemlock Cove. It was a beautiful spot.

"You're right, she's probably there," Clove was breathing heavily.

"Where's your car?" I asked.

"Thistle has it," Clove said.

"How did you get here?"

"Brian dropped me off on his way to the paper."

Crap.

I walked back up to the phone, took a deep breath, and then started to dial.

"Who are you calling?"

"We don't have a lot of options," I grimaced when I heard the voice on the other end of the phone. "Thistle is having a picnic with Marcus right now."

"I'll pick you up in five minutes," Landon said grimly.

TWENTY-SIX

"Where is this overlook?" Landon asked when we were all in his car and on our way back out to the inn.

"It's on the very back of the property," I explained. "It's like a mile from the clearing we were in the other night."

"Can we drive there?" Landon was grim, but I could tell he was trying to maintain an even keel. He was trying really hard not to panic us – which was having the opposite effect and completely freaking me out.

"No, not all the way," I replied, gripping the fingers on my left hand with those on my right nervously. "We'll have to park and walk the rest of the way."

"And how long will that take?" Landon glanced at me carefully.

"If we hurry, it shouldn't take more than ten minutes," I said, averting my gaze from Landon worriedly.

I directed Landon to the closest spot to park. When he had stopped the car, he turned to me expectantly. "What are the odds that you two will stay here in the car and just tell me how to get to this overlook?"

He must be joking. "Zero."

"That's what I thought," Landon blew out a sigh. "Come on."

Clove and I hurriedly started climbing the hill that led to the overlook. Landon was right behind us, but he didn't look thrilled with our configuration. "Let me be in front," Landon argued.

"Why?"

"I'm the one with a gun," he said simply.

Clove and I exchanged a look. "He has a point," she said.

We separated and let him in front of us. We watched him expectantly. "Well, where do I go?" He barked.

"How can you be frustrated with us?" I grumbled. Landon took off in the direction I pointed.

"How far?"

"About a mile."

"Why do I feel that going into the wilderness with you two is a bad idea?"

"I have no idea," I replied angrily. "If I realized you were going to be this big of a baby, I would have called Chief Terry."

"Why didn't you?" Landon had set a quick pace, but he slowed slightly when he asked the question. He obviously wanted to hear my answer.

"I don't know," I admitted truthfully. "You were the first person who popped into my mind."

Landon sighed. "Under other circumstances, I might find that flattering. Since we may be going to save your cousin from a possible murderer, I can't decide how I feel about that. I guess I'll figure it out later. Come on."

It didn't take us very long to get to the overlook – mostly because we all sensed the urgency of our endeavor. When we got close, Landon stilled us by holding up his hand in what looked like some weird military gesture. I swear, it was the exact same gesture Arnold Schwarzenegger used in *Predator* – and no, I don't watch too many movies.

"Wait here," he whispered.

"What? No," I protested wildly.

"Just let me make sure they're there and nothing bad has happened," Landon pleaded.

I blew out a frustrated sigh. "Fine."

Landon moved away from us, glancing back twice to make sure we were really staying where he had left us and not rushing off to certain death when his back was turned.

"We're waiting here?" Clove looked surprised.

"Of course not," I scoffed. "We're just waiting for him to move out of our sightline. Waiting here? Aunt Tillie would have a fit."

"Oh," Clove said in obvious relief. "I didn't think you'd just sit here."

When I was sure that Landon couldn't see or hear us, I led Clove around the other side of the bluff. There was a narrow path; rutted with roots and errant stones making the trek perilous, and we followed it until we came to the small clearing on the top of the bluff.

We pulled up short when we heard voices.

"What the hell are you doing, you freak?" Thistle sounded pissed. "Are you trying to kill me?"

Clove and I charged into the clearing ready to do great bodily harm to Marcus – with our bare hands if need be -- but stopped when the scene before us became clear. Thistle and Marcus were stretched out on a blanket on the ground. Thistle's hair was obviously mussed – and while her shirt was still on, her bra was cast to the side of the blanket haphazardly. They were both in a sitting position and glaring at Landon, who had pulled his gun and had it trained on the two of them.

"Are you going to shoot him?" Clove asked.

"For what? Taking her bra off in a public place?" Landon holstered his gun, but he was still watching Marcus suspiciously.

"What are you all doing here?" Thistle asked angrily, swiveling her head from Landon on one side to Clove and me on the other.

"Saving you," I offered lamely.

"From what? An orgasm?"

Marcus' cheeks reddened in embarrassment. I couldn't help but notice Landon was suddenly looking in any direction but Thistle's as well.

I opened my mouth to say something, but I didn't know what to say so I turned to Clove for help. "We were worried he brought you up here to kill you," Clove admitted.

Yep, that would help.

Landon rolled his eyes. I thought I heard him mutter the word 'unbelievable,' but I couldn't be sure.

"Why would Marcus try to kill me?" Thistle asked in abject disbelief.

"Well," I hedged. "Marcus' father served with Myron in Iraq and we thought he might have been involved in the gold heist," I blurted out.

Landon shook his head dramatically. "Don't tell him that."

"Why? It's the truth."

"So you think that I killed Myron for money I didn't even know about?" Marcus looked shocked. "I thought that was always some weird town rumor. Why would I possibly think that was real?"

"No," I said hurriedly, shrinking under Thistle's venomous glare. "I just ... I just ... ."

"You just overreacted," Thistle supplied. "Like you always do."

"I might have overreacted," I admitted sheepishly. "I just got worried when I called the inn and my mom said you guys went off on a picnic."

"You told your mom?" Thistle looked furious again. "She'll tell my mom and we're going to have an international incident on our hands, you idiot!"

"She was just looking out for you," Landon interjected. "You should be happy she cares enough not to let you die. Given your attitude, I would have just let you come up here with a murderer."

"Yeah," Thistle barked out sarcastically. "That's just what I was thinking."

"I'm not a murderer," Marcus said quietly.

"Of course you're not," Thistle patted his hand sympathetically.

"We have three suspects," Landon said calmly. "Marcus is one of them."

"Who are the other two?" Thistle asked.

"Ken Trask and Brian Kelly," I supplied.

"Why are you telling them that?" Landon asked in obvious frustration.

I shrugged. I told them everything. It had never occurred to me not to tell them, quite frankly.

Thistle considered it a minute. "It has to be Brian Kelly. He's a tool."

"That's what I said," Landon agreed. "We were questioning him when Bay called and said you'd been kidnapped."

"I did not say she was kidnapped," I rounded on him angrily. "Don't exaggerate. You were as worried as I was."

Landon shrugged noncommittally. "I still blame you."

Whatever.

A sudden commotion on the path behind us caused everyone to shift their attention in that direction. I wasn't surprised to see my mom and aunts – Aunt Tillie included – come rushing into the clearing. I was surprised to see Aunt Tillie holding a pitchfork, however. Where the Hecate had she found that?

"Unhand her, you rogue," Aunt Tillie ordered, brandishing the pitchfork in Marcus' direction threateningly.

"It's okay, Aunt Tillie," I said tiredly. "Marcus isn't trying to kill Thistle." At least we didn't think so at this point.

"Where did you get that?" Landon asked, looking at the pitchfork.

"We were in a hurry," Aunt Tillie sniffed. "I couldn't remember where I hid my gun."

"You have a gun?" Landon asked in disbelief. "What moron would give you a gun?"

"I did," Aunt Tillie said, casting a dark look in my mother's direction. "Someone hid it on me, though."

That was probably a smart move.

"Do you have a permit for a gun?" Landon asked. I didn't think he wanted a truthful answer to that.

"Don't you worry about that, copper," Aunt Tillie shot back. "It's none of your concern."

"As a member of law enforcement, it *is* my concern," he corrected her. "You have to have a permit for a gun, and if you have one, then someone should lose their job because they clearly don't know the parameters for giving out gun permits."

"Are you telling me you would take away an old lady's only source of protection?" Aunt Tillie challenged him. It was hard to find her scary with the ridiculous sunglasses, though.

I glanced at Landon to see if he would back down. It could go either way at this point.

"You don't look like you need a gun," Landon pointed out, gesturing to the pitchfork, which was still cocked in Marcus' direction.

"I improvised."

"I guess I should just be happy that you can't get a car up here, or you would have run him over," Landon grumbled.

I turned to my mom and aunts expectantly. "What are you guys doing here?"

"You told us Thistle was in danger. We figured out she was up here and came to save her," my mom said simply.

"I didn't say she was in danger," I said. "I said I needed to find her."

"No, you said she might be picnicking with a murderer," my mom countered. "Don't try to pretend you didn't. You overreacted and now you're trying to blame it on us."

"I did not!"

"She has always been an alarmist," Marnie explained to Landon. "As a child she was convinced Bigfoot was in the woods and refused to get near them for three straight months."

"Wasn't that after she saw the Bigfoot episode of *MacGyver*?" Twila asked.

"I think so," Marnie nodded.

"It was worse when we took her to the ocean and she wouldn't even put a toe in because she was convinced *Jaws* was going to eat her," my mom supplied. "That was the worst vacation ever."

"Do you guys have to tell him all of my embarrassing stories?"

"These aren't even the worst," my mom reminded me knowingly.

"Yeah," Marnie agreed. "We didn't even tell him how you were convinced you could turn into the Hulk and smash Aunt Tillie if you just got mad enough when you were ten."

I still hadn't been proven wrong on that.

"Or how about the time she thought the China doll was stalking her?" Twila giggled.

"It was!" I rounded on Twila angrily. "It was watching me when I slept."

"You just didn't like it because Clove told you that old ghost story about a China doll scratching eyes out and you freaked," Marnie said.

"It was watching me," I explained to Landon.

"She started hiding it all over the house," my mom said. "I would find it in the hamper, in the cupboards, in the closets."

"And you kept putting it back in my room," I said bitterly.

"I thought you would get over it," my mom clucked suspiciously. "Finally, one day, we came home and found her beating its face in on the pavement in front of the inn."

Landon glanced at me. "You killed the doll?"

"It was evil."

"It was an antique," my mom corrected me.

"Then you should have taken better care of it."

"Aunt Tillie told her it was cursed," Thistle interjected, suddenly remembering. "She told her that the doll could eat her soul during the night if she wasn't careful."

"Bay thought it was true because the doll looked exactly like her," Clove agreed. "It was a creepy doll."

"Why would you tell her that?" My mom turned on Aunt Tillie. "You know she freaks out over the strangest things?"

"She was bugging me when I was watching my stories," Aunt Tillie looked away quickly. "I was just trying to get her to shut up."

"I put that thing in the compost bin and it still showed up back in my room," I said angrily. "It was evil."

Landon shook his head. "It's over now. Let's move on."

Aunt Tillie finally lowered the pitchfork and turned to Thistle seriously. "I'm glad you weren't murdered."

"I'm glad I wasn't murdered, too," Thistle grumbled.

My mom still wasn't done with the China doll conversation. "Aunt Tillie kept finding the doll and putting it back in your room. It's not like it walked back in your room on its own."

"She said she wasn't," I protested.

"And you believed her?" Marnie asked. "It's your Aunt Tillie. Where do you think you three learned to lie so well from?"

I knew it!

"Why aren't you wearing a bra?" Aunt Tillie asked suddenly, trying to divert my wrath and direct attention back to Thistle.

"She's not wearing a bra?" Twila looked scandalized. "In public?"

Thistle turned to me darkly. "I'm going to make you pay for this. You think that doll was bad? You haven't seen anything yet."

TWENTY-SEVEN

Once everything had settled down, which took a lot of effort, Clove left with Marcus and Thistle, and my mom and aunts decided to walk back to the inn, leaving Aunt Tillie with me.

"Why aren't you taking her *with* you?" I whined.

"She shouldn't have to walk all that way back," my mom pointed out. "She's elderly. It's not good to tire her out for no good reason at her age."

"You just want a break from her," I grumbled.

Aunt Tillie reached up and smacked me on the back of my head. "Respect your elders."

Landon smiled despite himself. "It's probably a good idea for her to go with us anyway," he said. "It will give me a chance to talk to her about her gun."

Aunt Tillie looked suddenly uncomfortable. "Maybe the walk back would be good for me."

"Oh, it's too late for that," Landon said, leading her down the path and in the direction of his car.

"Fresh air is good for the body," Aunt Tillie said.

"I thought you were allergic to oxygen," Landon said, glancing pointedly at her sunglasses.

"Only my eyes are," Aunt Tillie reminded him.

"I wouldn't feel right about letting you walk back when I can drive you and make sure you get there safely," Landon said with faux sweetness.

I followed the two of them grumpily. This just wasn't my day.

When we finally made it back to Landon's car, he hadn't made any headway with Aunt Tillie regarding her firearm. He was clearly getting frustrated. "I still don't understand why you feel you need a gun?"

"I'm an old woman," she said. "I've made a lot of enemies through the years. I have the right to protect my family."

"Aren't most of them dead?" Landon asked blandly.

"What are you saying?"

"I'm saying you don't need a gun," Landon said matter-of-factly.

"I can't find it anyway," Aunt Tillie said. "Don't worry about it."

Landon shook his head, opening the door and helping Aunt Tillie into the front seat of the car. He shut the door and turned to me before I could get into the backseat. "How do you live with her?"

"I don't. I live in the guesthouse," I pointed out.

"You know what I mean."

"You'll get used to her."

"That's a frightening thought."

"At least she won't try and terrorize you with an evil doll," I sputtered.

"I still can't believe you were scared of a doll," Landon chuckled.

"You're scared of the dark," I reminded him.

"I'm not scared of the dark. I just don't like enclosed spaces."

Whatever.

When we were all in the car, Aunt Tillie turned to me expectantly. "Your mom told me why you suspected Marcus."

"Yes, I know, I jumped to conclusions," I sighed, leaning back into Landon's leather upholstery. "I don't need you to tell me that I'm an alarmist."

"I don't care about that," Aunt Tillie waved away my statement dismissively. "Your first inclination was to save your cousin. I can't fault you for that."

"You can't? Since when?"

"Don't be smart."

"What were we talking about again?"

"Myron."

"Oh, yeah, what were you saying?"

"I think you're on the right track with Brian Kelly," she said.

"Why?" Landon asked, his eyes keen.

"She just doesn't like him," I explained to Landon. "She thinks he's a tool."

"Does anyone like him?" Landon asked honestly. I saw his eyes shift up to the rearview mirror so he could gauge my reaction.

I kept quiet about Clove's crush. "Probably not."

"He's got a personality defect," Aunt Tillie said.

"What personality defect?" I asked.

"It's called narcissism."

That was true.

"That still doesn't explain why you think it's him?" Landon prodded Aunt Tillie carefully. I think she made him nervous. It would be ten times worse when he actually got to know her.

"She doesn't really think it's him, she's just hoping it's him so he'll leave the inn," I supplied.

"Don't tell me what I really think," Aunt Tillie glared at me. "I think it's Brian because Myron was William's son and if Brian knows that, he might have killed Myron to keep that little family secret quiet forever."

"What?" I asked incredulously. "William was Myron's father? How do you know that?"

"It was common knowledge," Aunt Tillie said. "William never claimed him publicly, but everyone around back then knew it. William had a wandering penis. He slept with half the women in town."

I thought about it a second. William and Myron did kind of look alike. "But why didn't William claim him? And you didn't sleep with him, did you?"

"He was married," Aunt Tillie said simply. "Myron's mother was a good woman, but she had a little problem. And I was a happily married woman. I would never cheat on your Uncle Calvin."

"What problem?"

"She was a nymphomaniac."

I looked at Aunt Tillie doubtfully. "A nymphomaniac? Do you even know what that is?"

"It's a woman that has a lot of sex," Aunt Tillie explained.

"That's a slut," Landon interjected. "Not a nymphomaniac. Sluts are a dime a dozen, but finding a true nymphomaniac is like finding a unicorn."

"We don't use words like that in this family," Aunt Tillie chided him.

"Sorry," Landon said sheepishly, averting his gaze from mine – which had darkened over the nymphomaniac joke.

Aunt Tillie turned to me. "Is he always such an asshole?"

"He's just trying to do his job," I replied. "You should let him do it."

Aunt Tillie harrumphed, but lapsed into silence as Landon drove. When we got to the inn, he turned to Aunt Tillie. "Don't tell anyone what you just told us," he ordered. "We need to do some research to find out if it's actually true or not."

"You can't tell me what to do," she said.

"I'm not telling," he corrected himself. "I'm asking nicely."

"It doesn't sound like you're asking nicely," Aunt Tillie argued.

Landon looked to me for help. "She won't tell anyone," I promised. I didn't believe it for a second, though. I knew the minute she made it into the inn she would blab to my mom and aunts. I didn't tell that to Landon, though.

"Are you sure?" he asked doubtfully.

No. "Of course. Aunt Tillie is trustworthy."

Aunt Tillie paused as she was getting out of the car. "Despite the fact that you're an asshole, I'm starting to like you."

Landon smiled at her winningly. "That's the nicest thing you've ever said to me."

Aunt Tillie glanced at me as I slid into the spot she had just vacated in the front seat. "Hurt her and I'll set you on fire."

"You'll set me on fire?" Landon didn't look convinced.

"And I won't need matches to do it," Aunt Tillie said. "And I'll start with your balls."

Aunt Tillie shut the door and shuffled off toward the inn without a backwards glance.

"She's joking, right?" Landon looked hopeful.

I shrugged. I had my doubts, though.

Landon swallowed hard and continued to watch Aunt Tillie until she was safely inside of the inn. He turned to me when she had completely disappeared from sight. "She's not trustworthy, is she?"

"Not even a little."

Landon sighed and started the car, pointing it back toward town. "Your family is exhausting."

He had no idea.

TWENTY-EIGHT

*W*hen I woke up the next morning, it took me a few minutes to realize it was Friday already. I had returned to the office long enough to pick up my laptop the day before, but then I had spent the rest of the afternoon at Hypnotic filing stories.

Brian hadn't been at the office when Landon and I returned, but Landon said he didn't want me to hang around The Whistler alone until he'd had a chance to talk to Brian and eliminate him as a suspect. I had a feeling that conversation was going to equate to two peacocks preening until one of the peacocks claimed his dominance and molted all over the other one.

I had already done most of the work for the new edition, so I didn't really have that much to do Thursday. Since Thistle was cranky when she got back to the store – through no fault of mine, I maintain – I did most of my work in silence. The only noise in the room was the occasional ding of my telephone when Landon texted me to make sure I was where I said I would be.

After I had finished filing all my stories, and emailing the paginator with suggestions for the layout, I wasn't surprised to find Landon waiting outside Hypnotic for me. He offered to spend the night at the guesthouse to make sure Clove, Thistle and I were safe.

When I declined, he looked like he wanted to argue, but instead he merely agreed and made me promise that the three of us wouldn't leave the guesthouse unless we were together.

Now, with the bright light of day filtering in through my window, I was starting to suspect that Landon hadn't really wanted to stay at the guesthouse. He had something else he wanted to do – but he was genuinely torn regarding our safety. He was a decent guy. He was a *condescending* guy, but he was a decent guy.

When I went out into the living room, I found Thistle and Clove having coffee at the island in the kitchen. "How did you sleep?" Clove asked.

"Okay."

"I'm surprised," Thistle grumbled. "With all the suspects running through your head, I would have figured you would have been tossing and turning all night."

"I told you I was sorry," I shot back. "Would you rather Clove and I leave you alone with a possible murderer next time?"

"That would be great," Thistle said sarcastically.

"Let's all just agree that we overreacted – and now Thistle is being a pain," Clove interjected nervously.

Thistle and I both shot her dark looks.

"Fine," Clove sighed. "Let's all just be pissy with each other all day instead."

That sounded like a fine idea.

"What time are you going to town?" Thistle asked grudgingly.

"After I shower."

"Today is the big kickoff of the murder mystery," Thistle pointed out. "We're all expected to be in town for the first victim reveal."

"Is it your mom?"

"No," Thistle sighed. "She's the third victim. She doesn't die until tomorrow afternoon."

"That's bound to be ... entertaining."

Thistle grimaced. "Or really embarrassing."

There was that, too.

"So what exactly is going to happen today?" Clove asked.

"Haven't you read the updates from Mrs. Little?" Thistle teased. I could tell she had decided to try and push her anger aside – at least for now.

"She sends like three a day. I stopped reading them a week ago," Clove admitted. "If I wanted to read that much, I'd pick up a book."

"Today is a special picnic lunch, complete with a barbecue by Mr. Winkler and a speech by Mrs. Little," Thistle supplied. "Then, they're going to have live music and sometime, during the evening, the first victim is going to drop."

"Who is the first victim?"

"I have no idea," Thistle shrugged.

"Does anyone else think it's morbid to do this with Myron's death still hanging over us unsolved?" Clove asked.

"It's the Hemlock Cove way," I replied. "It's all about keeping the tourists happy. The tourists want a murder mystery and a murder mystery is what they're going to get. It doesn't matter that it's tacky."

"Please, the tourists think it's more exciting because of Myron's death," Thistle scoffed.

That was a sad truth.

The three of us spent a lazy morning showering and getting ready for the picnic. It was a sunny day, and even though fall was officially here, temperatures were expected to remain comfortable in the high sixties so we all dressed in simple jeans, shirts and hoodies.

We decided to ride together – mostly because I could hear Landon's admonishments in my mind if he heard we separated – and headed off to town as a unit. We parked behind The Whistler and walked to the town square.

"When are you going to open the store?" I asked Thistle.

"In a few minutes," Thistle said. "I want to look around first."

Hemlock Cove doesn't do subtle. The town square had been decked out in a full contingent of red and black streamers, and a frightening mural roll out on the bank wall.

"Who did that?"

"Thistle helped," Clove said proudly.

"You did?" I turned to Thistle in surprise. "When did you have time for that?"

"It didn't take long," Thistle said, although I could see her cheeks coloring under the praise.

"It's pretty cool," I said, stepping closer to get a better look. The tableau was actually pretty horrifying – but in an abstract art way. There were bodies scattered around on the ground, all with a varying array of disgusting injuries, and there was a maniacal killer standing in the center of the havoc. You couldn't see who the killer was, though, because he was wearing one of those grain sacks over his head with black eyes cut out. It was truly menacing.

"Where did you get the idea for this?"

"We have a whole wall full of horror movies," Thistle pointed out.

"It's beautiful," I admitted. "Horrific, but beautiful."

"Of course it's beautiful."

I turned to find Marcus sidling up to Thistle and slinging an arm around her shoulders. He dropped a kiss on the side of her head and then turned to me expectantly. "Is this all right, or do you want to frisk me first?"

"Ha, ha."

"I just don't want you to jump me if you think I make too many sudden moves," Marcus teased.

I was relieved he didn't seem to be holding a grudge. "I think I'll leave the frisking up to Thistle," I said.

"That's probably a good idea," Thistle snuggled into Marcus. They really were cute together.

"Isn't this awesome?"

I cringed when I heard the voice. I turned slowly, plastering a fake smile on my face, and greeted Brian Kelly with as much warmth as I could muster. It wasn't much. "I didn't expect to see you here today."

"Why not?" Brian seemed genuinely surprised by my statement. There was a decided chill in his eyes, though.

"I don't know," I said. "I figured you would be busy with your redecorating project."

"That can wait," Brian waved off my suggestion like it was the craziest thing he'd heard all day. "This is a big deal for the town. I'm part of the town now. I figured I should get to know as many of my neighbors as possible."

"That sounds like a great idea," I beamed with faux enthusiasm. I could only hope he would go meet his new neighbors right now – and leave us alone.

True to form, Brian didn't seem to pick up on social cues. "What do you think they're barbecuing over there? It smells delicious."

"Hot dogs and hamburgers," I said shortly.

Thistle shook her head subtly when she met my gaze. I think she was warning me not to tip my hand that we suspected him of being a murderer. I was so uncomfortable in his presence, though, that I just wanted to put some space between the two of us.

I took the opportunity to do just that when the bank manager, Mr. Trask, exited his building and plowed right into me.

"Oh, sorry, Bay," he apologized; steadying me so I didn't fall backwards. "I didn't see you there."

"Mr. Trask," I greeted him. "How is the banking business?"

"It never really changes, not in a town like Hemlock Cove," he admitted.

"So, crappy?" I was trying to be cute, but I think I was coming off as a little tense. I blamed Brian.

Mr. Trask shrugged. "It is what it is."

An idea occurred to me suddenly. "Have you met Brian Kelly?"

Mr. Trask looked like he wanted to be anywhere but here – I recognized the look on his face as a mirror to the look that was probably on mine – but he greeted Brian amiably. He was a businessman, after all.

"You're William's grandson? It's nice to meet you."

Thistle, Clove, Marcus, and I took the opportunity to put some distance between us and Brian, leaving the two men to chat. When we were safely away, Thistle rounded on me accusingly. "You can't treat him like dirt until we're sure he's done something," she reminded me. "Then we'll pound him into the dirt."

"He gives me the creeps."

"He's a tool," Thistle nodded in agreement.

"I think you're being harsh," Clove interjected. "I think he's nice."

"You think he's hot," Thistle corrected her.

"No," Clove argued. "He's never done anything to any of us. We shouldn't treat him like a criminal."

"You had no problem treating Marcus like a criminal yesterday," Thistle pointed out sharply.

"That was Bay's idea."

"You're dead to me," I muttered to Clove.

Thankfully, the conversation didn't have a chance to diminish any further than it already had. We were interrupted in the middle of what I was sure would be a riotous hair-pulling fiasco by the sound of my phone chiming with an incoming text. It was from Landon.

"What does it say?" Thistle asked.

"They identified the body in the cave," I said, still trying to wrap my mind around the one sentence text.

"Is it someone we know?" Clove asked worriedly.

"It was Myron's sister."

TWENTY-NINE

"I didn't know Myron had a sister, did you?" Thistle looked at me questioningly. I could see her mind working as fast as mine felt like it was toiling.

"No," I said honestly. I turned to Clove. "Your mom didn't mention him having a sister, did she?"

Clove shrugged helplessly. "I don't ever remember anyone mentioning Myron had a sister."

"Do we know her name?" Thistle asked.

"According to the text, it's Ellen."

"Ellen Grisham? That doesn't sound remotely familiar," Thistle mused. She glanced in Marcus' direction. "Did you know Myron had a sister?"

Marcus looked lost in thought. "Actually, I think my dad mentioned it at one time. I can't remember how it came up, though."

I realized I was still holding my phone, so I punched in the number to the inn and waited for someone to pick up. Thankfully, it was Marnie and not Twila who answered.

"Did you know Myron had a sister?"

"Who taught you phone etiquette?" Marnie griped. "You say 'hello' first."

I blew out a frustrated sigh. "Hello. Did you know Myron had a sister?"

"Of course I knew that Myron had a sister," Marnie said dismissively. "Everyone knew that."

"None of us knew that," I corrected her. "You never mentioned it."

"How am I supposed to know what you do and do not know? That would be a fulltime job – and I already have a fulltime job."

Where is a wall when you want to beat your head into one? "Marnie, what can you tell me about her?"

"She was a pretty girl," Marnie said.

"Well, that's important," I said sarcastically.

"She was shy. She was pretty close with Myron," Marnie continued, ignoring my rampant sarcasm.

"Was she older or younger?"

"Younger, but only like a year younger," Marnie said. I could hear her talking to someone in the background at the inn. When she came back on the line, she sounded distracted. "What were we talking about?"

"Ellen Grisham," I reminded her.

"Oh, yeah, I don't know what you want to know," Marnie continued. "It all happened a long time ago."

"What happened a long time ago?"

Marnie was talking to someone in the background again. When she came back to the phone, she was clearly irritated. "It's really busy here. I can't talk to you right now. Call back later."

"Marnie, wait … ."

The sound of the dial tone was my only answer. "She hung up on me," I said incredulously.

"You look surprised," Thistle said. "She's hung up on me three times in the past week alone."

"Yeah, but I was asking her about something important," I whined.

"It obviously wasn't important to her."

I continued to stare down at the phone, like I expected it to magically come alive with the answers I was looking for. Finally, I snapped out of my trance and looked up at the trio of faces watching me. "I'm going to run to the paper and see if I can dig up anything about Ellen Grisham."

"Do you think you'll be able to find anything in the archives?" Clove asked doubtfully.

"I don't know, but there may be someone there who can help," I said elusively.

"Who?"

Thistle stomped on Clove's foot, a move that wasn't lost on Marcus. "She's a reporter," Thistle said sharply. "She has sources."

Clove looked confused for a few more seconds, and then realization washed over her face. "Oh! Right!"

Marcus looked confused, but he wisely kept his mouth shut.

"I'll see you guys in a few minutes," I said as I started toward the paper.

"Should you be going alone?" Clove asked. "Landon won't like that."

"Well, last time I checked, Landon wasn't the boss of me," I said breezily. He really was going to be pissed, though.

Once I got to the paper, I looked around for Edith and William, but I didn't find either of them. I sat down in my office and booted up my desktop computer. I usually used my laptop, whether I was in my office or not, but I had left it back at the guesthouse.

I typed Ellen Grisham into a search engine, and waited for the results. Not surprisingly, very little came up – and absolutely nothing that I could be sure was actually her.

"What are you doing?"

I looked up to see Edith sitting in the chair across from my desk. "Did you know Myron had a sister?"

"Ellen," Edith supplied.

"Yeah. Why didn't you tell me?"

"I didn't know you didn't know," Edith said.

"What do you know about her?"

"Not much," Edith admitted. "I was already a ghost by then, remember? She didn't spend a lot of time at the paper and I didn't spend a lot of time outside of this building. Or any time, really."

"Yeah, but you were haunting the paper even then. You must have heard something," I prodded her.

"I don't ever remember hearing anything about her really," Edith said. "William told me that she tried to help Myron when he came back from the war. She was his only living relative, after all."

Except for William, if that little tidbit was true. "But she couldn't?"

"I don't think anyone could."

"What did everyone think happened to her?"

"What do you mean?" Edith looked confused.

"Her body was found in a cave the other day."

"A cave? Who found it?"

I had to remind myself that I hadn't talked to Edith in days. She was way behind on the gossip. That had to be killing her. "Clove, Thistle and I found it when we were out looking for the stolen money," I admitted.

"Did you find the money?" Edith looked interested. I had no idea why, it's not like ghosts could go on a shopping spree.

"No."

"But you found Ellen's body?"

"Yep."

"That can't be a coincidence," Ellen mused. "You don't think Myron killed her, do you?"

That thought hadn't actually occurred to me. I thought about it for a second, and then I dismissed it. "I don't think so. I do think someone who knew about the money did it, though."

"You're talking about William," Edith said stiffly.

"No, I'm not," I corrected her. "I don't think William was the only one who knew about the money."

"You don't?" Edith looked surprised – well, surprised for a ghost.

"Someone killed Myron after William was already dead," I reminded her. "And William is hanging around for a reason. Has he told you why?"

Edith averted her gaze from mine. "Of course not."

"You're lying."

"I'm not lying," Edith charged. "I'm just not sure it's my secret to tell."

I didn't remind her that denying knowledge of something when you really had knowledge of it was technically lying.

"Well, then you get William's transparent ass in this office," I ordered. "I need answers – and I need them now."

"There's no reason to yell," William chastised me as he popped into view. He'd clearly been eavesdropping, for at least a little while.

"Enough is enough, William," I said, trying to slow my heart rate after it had jumped in conjunction with his sudden appearance.

William sighed. "I knew this would come out sooner or later."

"You knew about the money?"

"Yes," he admitted. "How did you know that?"

"Myron told me."

"Myron? Was this before or after he died?" Edith asked.

"After."

"You've seen him?" William looked hopeful.

"I have," I nodded.

"How is he?"

"He's lucid," I said. "Much more lucid than I ever remember him being in life, actually."

"Of course," Edith clucked. "Ghosts can't get drunk."

"Did he ask about me?" William asked.

"He did," I acknowledged. "I would have thought he would come and try to find you. Especially since you were his father."

William visibly blanched. "How did you know that?"

"Aunt Tillie told me."

"Your Aunt Tillie is a gossip." Among other things. "She shouldn't have told you that."

"She says Myron didn't know, but I don't believe that's true," I plowed on. "I think you told him. I think you told him when he came back from the war. I think it was your way of trying to help him – but it just hurt him." I was going for broke here.

William looked lost. "I tried everything I could think of. He just didn't want to listen. I think he convinced himself that I was lying."

"Maybe that's what he needed to believe," I suggested.

"What do you mean?"

"It's easier to believe that the man he looked up to was lying to try and help him out rather than to believe that he abandoned him and never claimed him and treated him like he wasn't worth being his son," I pointed out.

William's face fell in obvious shame. "I wanted to claim him," William argued. "I wanted to be his father. His mother had already remarried, though. He was already someone else's son. What could I do?"

"I don't know," I admitted. "You should have done something, though."

"It's too late now," William sighed.

"It's never too late," I reminded him. "You weren't Ellen's father, too, were you?"

"No, of course not," William was shocked.

"What do you know about Ellen?"

"She was a good girl," he said. "She and Myron were close. She couldn't help him anymore than I could, though."

"Did she know about the money?"

"I don't know," William admitted. "I'm sure Myron told her at some point, though. I think she was already married to Ken by then, though."

"Ken?" I leaned forward in my chair in surprise. "Not Ken Trask?"

"Yeah. They got married about a year after Myron and Ken returned from the war," William said. "It didn't last long, though."

"And then what happened?"

"I don't know," William shrugged. "I don't think her marriage to Ken was all that happy. She left him after a year and moved away. She never even contacted poor Myron again. I think that's what really sent him over the edge."

"She didn't move away William," I said, jumping to my feet excitedly.

"Of course she did," William scoffed. "Ken told me she left him a note and said she wanted a new life and just disappeared."

"Her body was found in a cave at the Hollow Creek a few days ago."

The realization of my words washed over William. "No," he said shakily. "Ken is a good man. He wouldn't ... he couldn't ... oh, God."

THIRTY

I was in a hurry to find Thistle and Clove when I left the newspaper. Had I been thinking, I would have called Landon or Chief Terry and told them what I had found out. I figured both of them would be in town square, though, so I could tell everyone at the same time. That apparently wasn't in the cards.

"Hello, Bay."

I gasped when I saw Ken Trask standing outside of the newspaper. He was still dressed in his khaki pants and blue button-down shirt from earlier this afternoon. His face, though, his face was completely different. It was like he was wearing an evil mask – like that hateful China doll. Or maybe, and I suspected this was actually the truth, the mask he wore was the one that made him look normal.

"Mr. Trask, it's good to see you again," I lied. I was trying to keep my voice even, but I wasn't sure it was entirely working.

I glanced around, hoping to see anyone from town. Heck, I would have settled for a tourist at this point. Unfortunately, this was the one time no one was around the newspaper offices – because, of course, everyone was in the town square.

"Who are you looking for?" Ken asked.

"No one," I lied smoothly. "Can I help you with something? If you're looking for an advertising rep no one is here right now." I was trying to act like nothing was out of the ordinary.

"Actually, yes," Ken said, narrowing his blue eyes in my direction. "You can tell me where the money is."

So much for pretending this was just a normal conversation. "I don't know what you're talking about."

"Don't, Bay," Ken rubbed the bridge of his nose wearily. "I'm tired. You have no idea how tired I am. I'm not in the mood for your games."

I thought about crying out – but with the sound of the band playing from a few blocks away, I knew it would be a fruitless endeavor. Ken wasn't exactly an imposing figure, but he did have four inches on me --- and about fifty pounds. I didn't know if I could take him in a fair fight. Of course, Ken had no intention of making it a fair fight.

I saw him pull a long-handled knife from his pocket and push it toward my mid-section. When I felt the cold point touch my skin through my T-shirt, I shivered involuntarily. "I don't know where the money is," I said.

"I don't believe you," Ken said menacingly. "You and your cousins were down at the caves. I saw you. You're the reason I'm in this mess."

"Why?" I challenged him. "Did we force you to kill Myron?"

"I didn't want to kill Myron," Ken seethed. "If he wasn't such a useless drunk, none of this would have been necessary." Ken poked me with the knife again. "Now move."

"Where?"

"To your car."

"It's parked behind Hypnotic," I lied.

"Isn't that your car right there?" Ken pointed with the knife.

"Oh, yeah, I forgot."

"Get in," Ken ordered.

I took one last look around in the vain hope that I would find some help and then I did as I was told. Ken was obviously unhinged. If he killed Myron in the middle of town with a bunch of people only a few hundred feet away, he would have no problem doing the same to me.

"Where are we going?" I asked when we were both in the car.

"Back out to the Hollow Creek," Ken said.

"Why?"

"To find my money."

"I thought it was in the cave with Ellen," I said bitterly as I navigated my car away from town and my only chance at safety.

"It was in the cave," Ken said. "Myron moved it when he was drunk one night and couldn't remember where he put it."

"What makes you think it's out there?"

"Where else would it be?"

"Why did you guys put it in a cave anyway?"

"That was Myron," Ken said angrily. "He decided where to put the money. We wanted to spend it, but he said it was stolen money and it should go for something good."

"So you all stole it together? You, Myron, Bill Kelly Jr. and Mike Wellington?"

"Myron is the only one who stole anything," Ken corrected me. "When we got home, he told Bill and me about it. We agreed to help him."

"Help him?" I raised my eyebrow suspiciously. "I have trouble believing that. You just wanted the money for yourselves."

"And what's wrong with that?" Ken challenged me. "The money was already stolen. It wasn't doing anyone any good rotting in a cave somewhere."

"So why didn't you and Bill just take it?"

"Because Myron couldn't remember where he hid it," Ken replied disdainfully.

"Let me guess, you guys went out there to help him remember?"

"We tried," Ken said. "We were very patient with him. We spent decades looking for that damned money. Each time Myron would remember where he hid it, we'd go there and then he would remember he'd moved it again."

"That must have been frustrating," I said with faux sympathy.

"You have no idea," Ken said. I was disgusted to see he was using the knife to pick between his teeth when I glanced over at him.

"How do you know the money is even still out there?" I asked pragmatically.

"Where else would it be?"

"Why do you think I'll be able to find it?"

"You found Ellen," Ken said angrily. "You'll find the money. I have it on good authority your family has special abilities when it comes to things like this."

I ignored the comment about my family. "Why did you kill Ellen?"

"She was going to leave me," Ken said simply. "She said she was going to take Myron away from here and get him some help."

"And you couldn't have that if you were ever going to find the money?" I supplied.

"Exactly. Park here."

I killed the engine and looked to Ken expectantly. "I don't know what you expect me to do. We didn't find the money when we were out here before. I don't think I'll be able to find it now."

"I guess we'll find out," Ken said ominously. "I'm running out of time."

"Because they identified Ellen's body?"

Ken looked surprised. "I didn't know they had. I knew it was only a matter of time, though. I have you to thank for that, don't I?"

I guess he did. "You're welcome."

THIRTY-ONE

he trek from the road to the Hollow Creek was unbelievably hard – especially since Ken insisted on being one step behind me and every time I stopped to decide which direction to take he bumped into me with the point of his knife.

"I see you got a new knife," I said as a means of conversation – a really creepy conversation, granted, but a conversation all the same. Really, what else were we going to talk about?

"I have a whole set," Ken said. "I was sad to leave the one behind in Myron, but I was in a hurry."

"I bet," I said. "It took a lot of guts to kill him with everyone so close. " Or a whole lot of crazy.

"I didn't mean to do that," Ken said hurriedly. "He just wouldn't answer my questions and ... it was one of those spur of the moment things."

"A crime of passion?" I suggested.

"Yeah, a crime of passion."

"Like with Ellen?"

"No, I knew what I was doing with Ellen," Ken grimaced. "What a bitch."

"Everyone said she was a nice woman," I argued.

"Nice to everyone but her husband," Ken interjected.

Oh, he was one of *those*. "So, what? She didn't wait on you hand and foot?"

"She was more worried about Myron. Poor Myron. Myron was a drunk. That's what Myron was," Ken ranted. "Myron was a stupid drunk to boot. He had a million dollars in gold coins from Iraq, and he lost them."

"A million dollars?" That sounded unbelievable to me. "How do you know what it was worth?"

"It was an estimate," Ken said, catching himself before he tripped over a tree root. Too bad, that would have at least given me a chance to run. Maybe I would have gotten really lucky and he would have impaled himself on his own knife.

"So you don't know how much it's worth?"

"I've never actually seen it," Ken admitted. "Myron told us about the money after he hid it."

"How do you know it's even real then?"

"Why would he lie?"

"He was a drunk," I pointed out. "They lie."

"He wasn't lying about this," Ken said evenly. "Ellen saw the money once. She told me."

"Maybe she was lying, too?" I don't know what I was trying to accomplish. I was just buying time at this point. Time for what, I still didn't know. I was alone out here. Thistle and Clove weren't here to back me up. It was just Ken, his really big knife and me.

"The money is real," Ken said irritably. "And I'm the only one left who can lay claim to it. It's mine."

"What are you going to do with it?"

"I'm going to move away from this place."

"Where?"

"Some sunny beach that doesn't have an extradition treaty with the United States," Ken said simply.

"That sounds nice." I wouldn't mind being on a beach myself right now – and not the cool and dark beach of the Hollow Creek.

When we got by the waterfront, I turned to Ken for further direction. "Now what?"

"Find the money," Ken barked.

"How?"

"Do one of your witchy little tricks."

"What?" I feigned ignorance.

"Don't, just don't," Ken admonished me. "This whole town knows about your family. They know you're all odd. They know you do spells, and you curse people, and you make little potions in your cauldrons."

"You watch too much television," I muttered. "We don't do any of that. Well, Aunt Tillie curses people, but usually only people she's related to."

"Yeah, your Aunt Tillie is a nut," Ken agreed. "She's terrifying."

"You have no idea," I agreed. "Her wrath is terrible."

"It's a good thing I'll be gone before she finds out I'm the one who took you," Ken said. "I would hate to see what she would do to me." He seemed amused – and scared – at the mere prospect of Aunt Tillie's anger.

"If you think distance can still her wrath, you're deluding yourself," I warned him.

Ken looked momentarily flummoxed. "What do you mean?"

"Aunt Tillie's curses can't be stopped by an ocean," I said.

"I guess we'll just have to see about that, won't we? I don't have a lot of choices here," Ken said.

From his point of view, I could see his reasoning. Damn.

"So … ?"

"So what?"

"So cast a spell and find my money," Ken said snappishly.

"What spell would you like me to cast?"

"I don't know, something that helps you find stuff," Ken said.

"I call upon the ancient power to find the gold," I intoned. "Poof." I looked around haphazardly. "It didn't work."

"Was that a real spell?" Ken narrowed his eyes at me suspiciously.

"I don't know, you tell me. You seem to know about all this witchy stuff."

"Don't get snarky with me!"

"You're asking me to do something I'm not capable of doing," I argued.

"Well, who can do it? Can your cousins?"

I didn't like the look in his eyes. There was no way I was going to unleash crazy Ken on my cousins. "No. We're not witches," I said. "Not like you think. We don't have magical powers. We can't wiggle our noses and make things happen. This isn't *Bewitched* or *Charmed*."

"What's *Charmed*?"

"It was a television show about witches," I said irritably.

"What does that have to do with anything?"

"It doesn't," I replied. "I was just explaining that I can't make things magically happen – just because you want them to – like on television."

Ken regarded me, his gray eyes dangerously slitted in overt anger. "I just think you're not properly motivated."

What was that supposed to mean?

"You will be," Ken promised. "You will be."

I opened my mouth to ask him what he meant by that, but I realized too late what was about to happen. It was like it was happening in slow motion, and yet I was still incapable of stopping it. Ken raised his hand, and I could see a tree branch in it. Darkness overcame me at the exact moment I realized he was going to hit me with it.

Not again. Aunt Tillie would never let me live this down.

THIRTY-TWO

I probably have brain damage. That's the first thought that went through my head when I started to regain consciousness. I've passed out twice in the past six weeks – and now I've been knocked out. That can't be good.

The second thought was that the head blow had obviously rendered me blind. The third was that, even though I thought my eyes were open, they actually weren't. When I did open my eyes, I wasn't surprised to see Ken looming over me from my prone spot on the ground.

"Gah!"

"It took you long enough," Ken griped. "You were out for more than an hour."

I tried to struggle to a sitting position, but the endeavor was harder than it should have been since my hands were tied behind my back. What the hell? "Why am I tied up? And why did you hit me in the head, you *ass*?"

"You weren't being helpful," Ken said simply. "I had to motivate you to help."

"And you thought hitting me in the head and tying me up – and

leaving me on the ground with bugs crawling on me, ugh --
would help?"

"Sorry about the bugs," Ken said. He actually sounded sincere.
"Hitting you in the head was a necessary evil. I tied you up because I
figured you would wake up while I was gone. I had no idea that you
would stay out so long."

"I've had a problem losing consciousness lately," I admitted
ruefully.

"Maybe you have a tumor?" Ken suggested helpfully.

"That would be nice," I muttered. "Wait, you tied me up and left me
here? Why?"

"I had to get some help in persuading you to do what I want."

Crap. Had he gone back to town and grabbed Clove or Thistle? I
looked around the small clearing, hoping against hope that Clove and
Thistle were still safe. When my gaze landed on the individual Ken
had grabbed, I felt my heart sink.

"Well, this is just another grand situation you've gotten us in."

"Aunt Tillie," I grumbled. "You went to the inn and grabbed my
Aunt Tillie? Are you crazy?"

Ken rubbed his jaw tiredly. I couldn't help but notice that he had a
darkening spot between his ear and chin. Aunt Tillie must have put up
a fight. He was lucky she hadn't clawed his eyes out and served them
in a soup for lunch.

"I was actually hoping to get your mom or one of your aunts, but
they were busy in the front of the inn," Ken admitted. "I waited for a
half an hour, but they never came back. I had to settle for your Aunt
Tillie."

"That must have gone over well," I mocked him, glancing at Aunt
Tillie. She had been ridiculously quiet during this whole situation. She
was probably plotting something. Of course, I couldn't tell because
she was wearing those stupid sunglasses.

"She's got a lot of energy for an old lady," Ken said.

"Who are you calling *old*?" Aunt Tillie barked.

"I didn't mean any disrespect," Ken held up his hands in surrender.
He was scared of Aunt Tillie, this was good. Of course, I was scared of

her, too. Especially given the fact that she was being unusually quiet. I wouldn't want to be Ken right now. I wasn't thrilled with being me, either.

"This guy is an idiot," Aunt Tillie said, raising a gnarled finger and pointing it at Ken angrily. "You have no idea the rain of shit I'm going to bring down on you."

I had to give it to her; she was an imposing sight – despite the sunglasses.

Ken swallowed hard. "I just want my money."

"Your money? It was stolen money. You didn't steal it. Myron did. You're so lazy, you're trying to steal from a drunk who did all the hard work," Aunt Tillie admonished Ken in a raspy voice.

"That's not the point," Ken protested. "I put up with Myron's drunken ass for years with the promise of that money being dangled over my head for the entire time. That's my money. I earned it."

"How did you earn it?" Aunt Tillie challenged. "Did you try to help Myron with his drinking problem? Or did you kill the one person who was trying to help him? Your own wife. You killed your own wife. You're a dick."

"Do you have Tourette's?" Ken asked. "You're swearing like a sailor, and I've never even heard you so much as curse once before."

"What can I say? You bring it out in me."

"All your niece has to do is find my money," Ken growled. "That's all I'm asking for."

"How do you suggest she do that?"

"You can use one of your witchy tricks," Ken suggested. "She cast a spell earlier, but it didn't work. I don't think she was really trying, though."

"You cast a spell for this idiot?" Aunt Tillie turned toward me. She didn't look happy.

"No."

"I didn't think so," Aunt Tillie turned to Ken again. "She's a pain in the ass, but she's not stupid."

"Well, then you need to cast a spell to find my money," Ken hedged.

"No."

"I said you had to."

"No."

"What the hell?" Ken looked like he wanted to kill someone. "I'm the one with the knife. You do what I say."

Aunt Tillie crossed her short arms over her ample chest and fixed her jaw in a grim line. "No."

"Goddamn you," Ken took an ominous step toward Aunt Tillie. She didn't shift her position. I had to admire her – even though she's evil incarnate on a daily basis – she was especially persnickety today. Ken must have read the obstinate slope of her body, because he stopped moving toward Aunt Tillie and instead headed back toward me. He grabbed me by the back of my hair and pushed the knife toward my throat. "I will kill your niece if you don't help."

"If you even think about touching her, I'll shrivel your balls to the size of walnuts and turn them black," Aunt Tillie said evenly, but I could sense the tension that had suddenly come over her. "Then, when they fall off, I'll feed them to you."

Well that was a pleasant visual.

"Let her go!"

I was relieved when I heard the new voice. I couldn't turn to see who had entered the clearing behind me, but I felt his warmth the minute he stepped into the empty circle beside the creek. Landon.

Ken looked up in surprise. "Who are you?"

"I'm the man with the gun telling you that if you don't let her go, I'm going to shoot you," Landon said. His voice sounded deadly serious.

"And what? You brought the pixie twins as your backup?"

The pixie twins? Clove and Thistle.

Ken pulled me around so my back was to him and I was facing Landon. Clove and Thistle were standing behind him, and Thistle's hands were clenched at her sides. Clove was moving carefully along the outside of the circle in Aunt Tillie's direction. When she got there, she put her hand on Aunt Tillie's shoulder. "Are you all right?"

"I'm fine," Aunt Tillie grumbled. "He's the one who's going to be sorry. He interrupted my nap."

Yeah, that was the big crime of the day.

"How did you know I was here?" I asked Thistle.

"We had a little help," Thistle said. "Someone saw him forcing you into your car at knifepoint."

I met Thistle's hard gaze with uncertainty. Who could have possibly seen him taking me? Everyone was at the town square.

"Your friends from the paper saw," Thistle supplied.

Edith and William.

"And they found you at the celebration?"

How had Thistle and Clove heard Edith when I wasn't near? That had never happened before.

"They did. Then we found Landon," Thistle slid a glance at Aunt Tillie. "We had no idea he had her, too, though."

"Yeah, he was trying to motivate me to help," I said bitterly.

"He should have brought you a bag of candy then, instead of a bag of crazy," Thistle said.

"I won't forget that," Aunt Tillie warned.

"I know," Thistle sighed. "If anyone knows that, I do."

"Can we focus on the crazy guy with a knife to my throat instead of Aunt Tillie?" I asked.

Landon hadn't moved a muscle, I noticed. His gun was trained on Ken – and his gaze was fixed on the knife at my throat. "You have nowhere to go," Landon said. "There's only one option here. You surrender and go to jail. Or, you hurt her, and I'll kill you. That's if these three don't get to you first."

Ken looked around the circle in obvious fear. I couldn't tell if he was more scared of Landon and his gun or Aunt Tillie and her anger, though.

"I have a better idea," Ken suggested. "I take Bay with me. When I get far enough away, I promise I'll let her go."

"You killed your wife," Aunt Tillie argued. "Like we're going to trust you."

"I don't see where you have a lot of options," Ken said lamely.

"I was just going to say that to you," Aunt Tillie said, climbing to her feet menacingly.

"What are you doing?" Ken asked nervously, glancing at Aunt Tillie warily.

"I'm going to show you exactly what my anger is capable of," Aunt Tillie warned. "Let her go, or this is going to become a really dark world for you."

Ken started visibly shaking. I heard the gravel behind us crunch – despite the fear that was quickly overtaking me. I couldn't tell what was going on, though. All I knew was that Ken's grip on my hair had loosened as he turned to look behind him. Then I heard the sickening crunch of something crashing into his head this time.

"What the hell!" Landon exploded.

THIRTY-THREE

I took advantage of whatever crazy scenario was going on behind me to crawl away from Ken. The harsh ground dug into my knees through the denim of my jeans, but I pushed all thoughts of pain out of my head. I fell forward at Thistle's feet. She was on her knees working on the rope tying my hands within seconds.

"What's going on?" I gasped.

"You have to see it to believe it," Thistle said.

I felt my hands spring free and I jumped to my feet anxiously, almost toppling over when the blood started rushing to my feet for the first time in more than an hour. Thistle grabbed my arm for support.

When I turned around, I was stunned to see that my mom and aunts had joined the melee – and their way of helping was to conk Ken over the head with a big branch. I think it was the same one he had hit me with. That was poetic justice. Since my mom was holding it, I had a feeling she had done the deed herself. Landon kept trying to dart in between the arms and legs that were steadily beating Ken – I think Twila got a few kicks in, too – to get a handle on the situation.

He drew back suddenly when Ken reared up and grabbed Twila's arm and tugged her to him. Great. I was free, but he had a new hostage. Twila looked understandably petrified.

Marnie and my mom wisely took a step back. My mom raised the branch to hit Ken again, but Landon stilled her with a look. "Don't do that again."

"He's got my sister."

"If you hit him the wrong way, he could cut her throat," Landon warned.

"That didn't happen when I hit him when he had Bay," my mom argued.

"Just calm down," Landon snapped. He looked around at all of us wearily. "You're all unbelievable."

"How did you find us?" I asked them. My gaze was fixed on Twila's frightened stare.

"We weren't looking for you," Marnie said. "We knew something was wrong when Aunt Tillie wasn't on the couch for her afternoon nap."

"See," Aunt Tillie muttered. "I told you he interrupted my nap."

"Is that really important now?" Thistle looked infuriated at Aunt Tillie, but I could tell she was really scared for her mom.

"Okay, let's get a handle on this situation," Landon said calmly, although I could tell he was anything but calm. "Why don't you all take your Aunt Tillie back to the inn, and Ken and I will have a nice and civilized talk?"

Like that was going to happen.

"No," Aunt Tillie said obstinately. "Why don't you go to the inn and have a drink, and let us handle this?"

Landon looked at her in disbelief. "Are you kidding me? I'm the one with the badge. I'm the one with the gun."

"If you feel that's important, you can leave the gun with me," Aunt Tillie suggested. "You can keep the badge, though. That's not going to be any help. I promise I'll get the gun back to you when we're done here."

Landon shook his head in disbelief and turned his attention back to Ken. For his part, Ken looked like a sweaty mess. The trickle of blood running down the side of his face only made him look more unhinged.

"You know," Landon lamented. "This is the second time in six weeks that I've been in a situation like this – and it has almost all the same players."

"At least Ken's not a drug dealer," Clove said helpfully. "And he's alone. Last time, we had a lot more crazy people with guns."

"Yeah, that's exactly what I was thinking," Landon said sarcastically. "I don't know how you do it," he swiveled on me.

"Do what?" I grumbled, rubbing my wrists to restore circulation. It was a painful process, but I figured I might need my hands in the next few minutes.

"You find the exact worst situation in the world to get into," Landon continued. "It never occurs to you that it's a terrible idea. You just jump in headfirst and see how badly you can screw things up."

"How is this my fault?"

"Why didn't you call me from the paper?" Landon challenged.

"I was on my way to find you downtown," I said.

"No, you were on your way to find Clove and Thistle," Landon corrected me. "If you happened to run into me, then you would have told me, too."

"That is so ... well, true, but I was totally going to tell you," I said.

"After you told them?"

"Is that really important now?"

"Ken," my mom interrupted my little spat with Landon. "Just let Twila go. We'll tell the judge you weren't really going to hurt anyone."

"He killed Myron and Ellen," Aunt Tillie pointed out.

"You're not helping," my mom hissed through gritted teeth.

"I didn't know you wanted me to," Aunt Tillie sniffed.

"In what scenario – especially this one – would you think I wouldn't want you to be helpful?" I had heard that tone of voice before. Someone was in for an earful later tonight.

"Can we all focus on me?" Ken asked irritably.

"Of course," Aunt Tillie said amiably. That was a clear sign she was about to do something awful. "Let's focus on you, Ken."

Ken looked appropriately abashed. "Well, then, what about me?"

"There is no money, Ken," Aunt Tillie said evenly.

"What? That's not true," Ken sputtered.

"The money is gone. It has been for years."

"How do you know that?" He asked.

"Myron told me."

"When?"

"Yesterday."

Crap.

Landon looked surprised. "Yesterday," he interjected. "Myron has been dead for almost a week."

"Only his body is dead," Aunt Tillie said. "His soul is still lingering."

"I'm sorry, what?"

"You're saying he's a ghost?" Ken looked stunned.

"He is," Aunt Tillie said carefully. "And is he ever pissed at you."

"He told you that Ken killed him? Why didn't you tell us that?" I practically exploded.

"I forgot," Aunt Tillie shrugged.

I glared at her openly. "He didn't tell you that. You're making it up."

Landon looked at me doubtfully. "That's what you're incredulous about? That she's making up stuff from a ghost, not that she claims she's been talking to a ghost?"

Yeah, that was a conversation for another time – like hopefully never.

"He would have told me that, if he'd remembered," Aunt Tillie argued.

Whatever. "That's so not the point."

"Well then, what is the point?" Aunt Tillie asked irritably.

"Where is my money?" Ken screamed.

"I told you, it's gone." Aunt Tillie was nonplussed. "Myron moved it to that old cabin in the woods. It burned when the cabin did."

"They were gold coins," Ken argued. "They don't burn like paper money."

"Yeah, well no one found them," Aunt Tillie said. "Then the flood of 1998 washed the entire embankment away."

"No, no, no," Ken shook his head in disbelief.

"Yes," Aunt Tillie nodded smugly. "The money has been gone for almost fifteen years. You've been out here looking for something that doesn't even exist."

"How long have you known this?" Landon asked.

"I told you, since yesterday."

"That's impossible," Landon barked out. "Myron is dead. He's not a ghost."

"You don't know that," Aunt Tillie scoffed. "You just don't understand our ways."

"What ways?" Landon cast a dark look in my direction.

"Not now," Aunt Tillie said dismissively. "We have other things to deal with. Twila looks like she's going to pee her pants."

"And how do you, in your infinite wisdom, think we should deal with this?" Landon looked like he was going to spontaneously combust.

"No one needs your sarcasm," Aunt Tillie chided Landon. "I understand this is a difficult situation for you, but you've got to learn that there's a time and place for you to deal with your stuff. This is about Twila now. We need to worry about her stuff."

I heard Clove bite down a mad laugh behind me. The situation really had spiraled out of control.

"I really can't believe I'm in this situation," Landon complained.

"Welcome to my world."

Aunt Tillie straightened up, bringing all of her four feet and eleven inches of height to bear, and stepped in front of Ken. "Let her go, or I'll make you wish you had never been born."

"And how are you going to do that?" Ken asked caustically. "I hate to break it to you, but I'm already there."

"Things can always get worse," she said evenly.

"I don't see how," Ken said bitterly. "What are you witches going to do? Curse me? What could you possibly do to me that's worse than what I'm looking at right now?"

That was the dumbest question he had ever asked – or at least the dumbest question he had asked this afternoon.

AMANDA M. LEE

Aunt Tillie reached up and dramatically drew her sunglasses away from her face. Her usually brown eyes were tinged with red, and the atmosphere around us was suddenly sparking with invisible electricity that threatened to ignite the dusky sky itself.

I looked up at the previously clear heavens and saw the darkening clouds that were now rolling in and felt my stomach drop. *Oh shit.* The hairs on my arm were suddenly standing on end. She was going to do it. She was really going to do it.

"It's time for you to do one right thing in your life," Aunt Tillie said to Ken, taking another step toward him. "Let Twila go and take responsibility for yourself. For your actions. Stop blaming others."

Ken looked helpless. "I can't."

"How did I know you were going to say that," Aunt Tillie sighed. "Once a coward, always a coward."

"What are you doing?" Ken screeched. He was looking at the suddenly dark sky and I could tell that any sanity he had previously possessed had fled.

"What makes you think I'm doing anything?" Aunt Tillie asked. Her voice had dropped three octaves. She was going for scary, I know, but she was rapidly bordering on demonic.

"You're making it storm," Ken said accusingly.

"That's not possible," Aunt Tillie scoffed. "That would make me magic ... or something."

Or something was right.

"Bay, what's going on?" The alarm in Landon's voice tugged at my heart.

"It will be fine," I said soothingly. "I promise"

"But what's going on?"

"I don't know," I lied. "It's just one of those sudden fall storms."

"Sudden?" Landon's voice had gone squeaky. "This is more than sudden. It wasn't supposed to storm."

"It's her," Ken pointed at Aunt Tillie with his knife. "She's calling on the Devil to come and get my soul."

"The Devil has had your soul for a long time, Ken," Aunt Tillie said.

194

She was still using her scary voice. "Maybe he thinks it's just time to take payment of what is already his?"

"That's not helping," I hissed.

"Surrender now, Ken," Landon suggested. "Maybe the storm will go away if you do?"

"I can't surrender," Ken whined. "I can't go to jail. I won't survive in jail."

"He has prison bitch written all over him," Marnie said knowingly.

"Now you talk?" I glanced at her. "Now, when it's too late?"

"When what's too late?" Landon's voice sounded like he was miles away instead of feet.

I took a hesitant step toward Aunt Tillie. "Don't do this."

"We don't have another choice," Aunt Tillie said. "Ken is beyond reason. Can you see another way out of this? One that doesn't end with Twila's death?"

"We can talk to him," I pleaded. "We can work out a trade."

"You can't barter with crazy," Aunt Tillie said, turning back to fix her glowing eyes on me for a second. "You, of all people, should realize that."

"What is she talking about?" Landon asked.

Aunt Tillie's red eyes showed me a lot of things – including the sad truth: She was right. I took a deep breath and stepped back away from her.

"Do your worst," I nodded.

When the lightning struck, it was close. A blinding light filled the clearing and the sound of thunder was deafening. Everyone was thrown back by the shock of it all – and then everything went dark again.

And eerily silent.

THIRTY-FOUR

"Someone better tell me what just happened! Right now!"

I rolled over and saw Landon sitting on the ground a few feet away from me. He was looking in the direction where Ken had been just a few minutes before. Ken wasn't there anymore, though, and Landon was climbing shakily to his feet in disbelief.

I looked around in a blind panic for a second. Where was Twila? I was relieved to see her entwined in a pile of arms and legs with Marnie and my mom. They were all grumbling wildly.

"Get off me!"

Thistle and Clove were another few feet away from me, to my left, and they looked a little dirty but unharmed. Aunt Tillie was still standing where she had been before she'd opened the sky above us.

Landon was on his feet. He looked queasy, but he was towering over me as he grabbed my hand and pulled me up beside him. I basked in his warmth for a second – but the feeling didn't last. "What the hell is going on?"

"I don't know," I answered honestly.

"Really? Because you don't seem surprised that your Aunt Tillie threatened Ken with imminent harm and then a lightning bolt struck exactly where he was standing and your aunt, who was also standing there, is fine and Ken just seems to be gone?" Landon was breathing hard. I didn't blame him.

"I saw exactly what you saw."

Landon shook his head. "You know more than you're saying."

I brushed his hand away and hurried to Aunt Tillie's side. I was happy to see that her eyes had returned to normal. She didn't seem at all shaken by the events of the past hour.

"Are you all right?"

"I'm fine," she said dismissively. "I am ready for my nap, though."

THE NEXT WEEK was intense – to say the least. The murder mystery had gone on as planned – and all the tourists seemed to have a good time. Twila's death scene was a tour de force – or so I heard. I hadn't actually gotten a chance to see it. Landon and Chief Terry were questioning me – the former having maintained a steadfast distance since Ken's disappearance – while Twila was earning her Oscar in the town square.

Chief Terry seemed concerned by Landon's report of the day's events, but he had also seemed disinterested in following up on the matter. I think Chief Terry had an inkling of what had happened, but he knew he couldn't explain it so he was eager to bury it instead.

The official story said that Ken had disappeared in the confusion of the moment – but I knew better. I think Landon knew better, too, but he didn't want to admit it. He had been shaken when we left the clearing by the creek, but he had also been quiet. I didn't take his silence as a good sign.

After the dust had settled, I made up with Brian – or at least apologized for suspecting him of murder. He brushed off my apology, but I could tell his nose was still out of joint. I could only hope he didn't take out the aggression he was obviously feeling on the paper – or me specifically. I still had no idea why he had been searching William's office so relentlessly. I figured that was a mystery for another time, though.

Marcus and Thistle were lost in their own little world, and he had graciously accepted my apology for thinking that he was a killer – even though it was just for a few random minutes. He was now doing constant sleepovers. It was actually nice to have him around, though. He'd done a ton of home repairs in the past week. The guesthouse was looking better and better.

A few days after Ken had disappeared, I had caught a glimpse of Myron and William's ghosts walking through town together. They had looked happy, like they were catching up on old times. It was about time.

Edith had told me that they had passed on together a few days after that. I guess William's unfinished business had nothing to do with the money and everything to do with his son. When his autopsy came back, it turned out he had died of natural causes after all. At least Ken didn't have William's blood on his hands as well.

Ellen was laid to rest next to her brother – with her maiden name and not her married name. I could only hope she had passed over a long time ago. I was sad to think of her wandering around Hemlock Cove for decades alone.

Since it was Friday, and I had just sent the new edition to the paginator, I found myself walking up to the inn alone. Clove and Thistle were already there – at least that's what the note at the guesthouse said – and they warned me that Aunt Tillie was on a rampage, so I shouldn't be late. What else was new?

When I climbed the hill that led to the backdoor of the inn, I was surprised to find Landon waiting for me on the back patio.

"What are you doing here?"

"I knew you'd be coming up for family dinner," he said simply. I couldn't help but notice he kept a few feet of distance between us.

"How did you know that?"

"Clove told me when I stopped by Hypnotic today."

I watched Landon curiously. He looked uncomfortable. "I haven't seen much of you over the past week – except when you had me hauled into the police department to answer questions during Twila's big death scene."

"I'm sure that upset her."

"I'm still paying for it." She'd made me weed her gardens. I hated gardening. I couldn't be sure, but I think Aunt Tillie had enchanted it so the weeds regrew every day. I wasn't exactly making any progress.

"I needed some time to think," Landon admitted.

"About what?"

"You. Your family."

"You probably need more than a week," I said.

"I need to know what happened to Ken." There was a pleading tone to Landon's words.

"I don't know what happened to Ken," I said sharply. "I told you that. I saw what you saw."

"But you weren't surprised."

"I was in shock," I corrected him. "We were almost just struck by lightning. I was processing."

"But you weren't surprised," he repeated.

"I don't know what you want me to say," I said helplessly.

"I know you're hiding something, Bay," Landon replied. "You either can't or won't tell me, though."

"And what do you think I'm hiding?"

"It has something to do with your family," Landon said. "And it's more than that pot field your aunts are hiding out in the woods."

"You know about that?"

"I saw it the night I stumbled on your little ritual."

Ritual. That was an interesting – and apt – word.

"Are you going to report them?"

"No," Landon sighed. "I don't want to get on your Aunt Tillie's bad side. I have a feeling that wouldn't be in my best interests."

"Probably not."

I had remained a few feet away from Landon for the duration of our conversation – even though I had wanted to move closer to him. From this distance, I couldn't feel his warmth. Even if I was closer, though, I had a feeling that the coldness emanating from him would envelope me instead of the warmth I sought.

"I like you," Landon said finally. "You're funny. You're weird.

You're ridiculously loyal. You're also hiding something from me. I need you to trust me and tell me the truth."

I bit my lower lip. If I did tell him the truth, I ran the risk of scaring him away forever. He would also then know our secret. I didn't know what he would do with it, but I couldn't take the risk of telling him. It wasn't just my secret, after all. I remained silent, even though I could feel my heart restricting in my chest.

"You're not going to tell me, are you?"

"I don't ... I ... I don't have anything to tell you," I said lamely. "I can't give you what you're looking for."

"I guess not," Landon said glumly.

We lapsed into an uncomfortable silence again. It didn't last long.

"I thought I heard voices."

I turned to see Aunt Tillie standing on the patio behind me. She was giving Landon one of her patented glares. Ever since the day at the Hollow Creek, she had stopped wearing her sunglasses. She said her allergy had been cured by the sudden storm.

"Aunt Tillie," Landon greeted her wanly.

"Are you coming in for dinner?" She asked him pointedly.

Clove and Thistle had wandered out to the patio after Aunt Tillie. They were watching the situation with great interest – and they were listening for the answer as well.

"Not tonight," Landon said, forcing a smile in my direction. "Maybe some other night. I've got some things to think about. I've got some things to do."

"Well, you should go do your important things then," Aunt Tillie said crisply. "We don't want anyone here that doesn't want to be here."

Landon met Aunt Tillie's heavy gaze. "I'm going."

Aunt Tillie took a step toward him, never letting her gaze waver from his face. "And remember, we may forgive, but we never forget."

Aunt Tillie grabbed my hand and started pulling me away from Landon. I let her pull me, not looking back at Landon despite the lump in my throat. "When have you ever forgiven someone?"

"Stranger things have happened," she said soothingly. "Don't worry, dear. He'll be back. He's a man. They have to figure things out on their own. And, since he's a man, it will take him twice as long as it would take a woman."

I could only hope she was right. Despite myself, I missed him already. "How can you be sure?"

"If he's not, I'll just curse him until he wishes he made the right decision from the beginning," she said simply. "They always come back, dear. We're like a fine wine. We're addictive – and he's already addicted. He won't know until he starts to go through withdrawal, though. It won't take long."

"I hope it hurts," Thistle said grimly.

"It will," Aunt Tillie promised. "You can be sure of that."

CPSIA information can be obtained
at www.ICGtesting.com
Printed in the USA
LVOW13s1657100718
583149LV00009B/1095/P

9 781483 981277